W9-CCT-677

THE
DEVIL'S
SHARE

THE DEVIL'S SHARE

Wallace Stroby

Minotaur Books
New York

THE DEVIL'S SHARE. Copyright © 2015 by Wallace Stroby. All rights reserved. Printed in the United States of America. For information, address St. Martin's Press, 175 Fifth Avenue, New York, N.Y. 10010.

www.minotaurbooks.com

Designed by Steven Seighman

Library of Congress Cataloging-in-Publication Data is available upon request.

ISBN 978-1-250-06575-9 (hardcover)
ISBN 978-1-4668-7275-2 (e-book)

Minotaur books may be purchased for educational, business, or promotional use. For information on bulk purchases, please contact the Macmillan Corporate and Premium Sales Department at 1-800-221-7945, extension 5442, or write to specialmarkets@macmillan.com.

First Edition: July 2015

10 9 8 7 6 5 4 3 2 1

Fear begins where desire ends.

—Baltasar Gracián

This American system of ours, call it Americanism, call it capitalism, call it what you like, gives to each and every one of us a great opportunity if we only seize it with both hands and make the most of it.

—Al Capone, interview with journalist Claud Cockburn, Chicago, 1930

THE
DEVIL'S
SHARE

ONE

With dusk, the setting sun turned the ocean to fire. Crissa stood on the balcony and looked out across the hills, the houses there almost hidden by the trees. Through the haze, she could see all the way out to the beach and the amusement pier, the darkening water beyond. Up here, the traffic noise from Santa Monica Boulevard was just a hum.

A breeze stirred the trees below, the scent of night-blooming jasmine rising up. She looked down over the ornate marble railing. A thirty-foot drop and a flagstone patio there, surrounded by a lush garden, willow trees. A stone fountain in the middle, water tinkling gently.

"Million-dollar view," Hicks said behind her.

She turned as he came out on the balcony. The French doors were open, the curtains moving in the breeze.

"More than that, I'd guess," she said.

He was in his early thirties, lean and fit, dark hair cropped short, a two-days' growth of beard. He'd been waiting for her when she'd walked out of the terminal at LAX and into the afternoon heat. She hadn't been happy when she saw the car, a gleaming black four-door Jaguar. A vehicle like that would stick out, turn heads. But she'd kept her mouth shut as he put her overnight bag in the trunk, held the passenger door for her.

He'd worn a shirt and tie at the airport but now was in stone-washed jeans, a tight black T-shirt. There was a tattoo on the inside of his left forearm, a green-and-red snake curled around a dagger.

"He's ready to see you now," he said. "I mean, if you're ready."

She looked west again. The sun was all but gone, the gardens below and the trees downslope lost in shadow. The boulevard was a long line of red taillights.

She followed him through the doors and into a big room with an oak worktable in its center, paintings on the walls, the domed ceiling lost in shadow.

She stopped in front of a lithograph of a wolf, its head back, howling into darkness.

"You know art?" he said.

She shook her head.

"But you know what you like?"

"Sometimes."

They went down a flight of stairs to a marble-floored room, a stone fireplace on one side, a grand piano on the other. Art on all the walls, sculptures on pedestals. There was another set of open French doors, the breeze coming through, bringing the smell of the garden.

The man who came in from the balcony was in his late sixties, longish white hair combed straight back, beard neatly trimmed. He wore a white suit, a pale pink silk shirt open at the neck. His cane tapped the floor as he approached. It was gnarled and thick, would be a weapon in the right hands.

"I'm sorry to keep you waiting," he said. "Some last-minute business to attend to before I was free to talk." He gave a small smile, extended his hand. "I'm Emile Cota. Thank you for coming."

She took his hand, saw the liver spots, felt the thin skin, the bones beneath. He waved the cane at a trio of wide, cushioned club chairs around the fireplace. "Shall we sit? Talk? Randall, can you find Katya, have her pour some drinks for us? She's back there in the pantry somewhere. Macallan for me and . . ." He looked at her.

"Nothing, thanks," she said.

"As you will. But please, sit." He swept a hand toward the chairs, the stone-and-wood coffee table there. Hicks left the room.

She looked around, not liking what she saw. A house like this, with so much art, would have hidden cameras, alarms. Maybe a room somewhere with CCTV screens, someone watching.

"What's wrong?" he said.

"I'm not sure this is a good idea."

"You haven't heard what I have to say yet."

"I meant coming here."

"But you have, haven't you? So, let's build from there."

She took the chair closest to the door. He waited for her to sit, took the center one himself, facing her at an angle. He laid the cane across his lap. "I appreciate your agreeing to meet like this."

There was nothing to say to that. And nothing she could do to speed him up. He'd tell it in his own time.

"You come highly recommended," he said. "At least as far as our friend in Kansas City is concerned."

That was Sladden, the contact man she sometimes used as a go-between. It was Sladden's call that had gotten her out here. The details he'd given had been minimal, but enough to whet her interest. More than a year since she'd last worked, and she was bored, restless.

"So, Ms. Wynn, is it? How do you prefer to be addressed?"

Christine Wynn was the name she was using here, the one Sladden had given him. It was on the driver's license and credit cards she carried.

"Christine's fine," she said.

Hicks came back into the room, holding a short, square glass with brown liquid, a single ice cube inside. He swirled the drink, took the chair to Cota's left. In his wake came a blond woman in a white smock, carrying a silver tray. She was in her forties, attractive in a hard way, hair tied back. On the tray was a drink identical to the one Hicks had, a bottle of scotch with a blue label, an ice bowl with tongs, and a green bottle of Perrier.

She set the tray on the table without a word, unscrewed the Perrier cap.

"I had her bring that anyway," Hicks said. "Thought you might want to hydrate after your trip."

"Thanks," Crissa said. She didn't touch it. Her hands were bare, and she wouldn't chance fingerprints.

Cota said, "Thank you, Katya. I think we'll be fine for the rest of the evening."

She cut a glance at Crissa, then left the room. Crissa watched her go.

"Ms. Wynn was just telling me she wasn't altogether comfortable coming here," Cota said. "I'm hoping to reassure her."

Hicks nodded, sipped his drink.

"Feel free to talk," Cota said to her. "Randall here is my *facto factotum,* so to speak. He's an employee in the strictest sense. But I trust him like a son. He knows all my business."

"Who lives here?" she said.

"Just myself. I have visitors from time to time, but no one stays very long."

"What about Katya?"

"This monstrosity has more than its share of guest rooms. She stays here three or four days a week. I get along on my own the rest of the time."

"Should have given her the night off," Crissa said.

"Ah," Cota said. "It crossed my mind. But Katya has worked for me for many years. I'm sure she's learned to forget what she sees here. Not that there's ever much to see." He lifted his glass, tilted it at her and drank.

"All this art," she said. "You must have a security system. I'm guessing the house is wired for sound. Video, too."

"Alarmed, yes. Wired, no. I certainly wouldn't want a permanent record of everything that goes on in this house, would I?" He smiled.

"I know I wouldn't," Hicks said.

"There's no need to worry on that front, believe me," Cota said. "And we're just getting acquainted here anyway."

He had a faint accent she couldn't place. European, but sanded down by years in the States.

"How was your flight?" Hicks said, and grinned.

"It was fine." Returning the undercurrent of sarcasm in his question. They hadn't known where she was coming from, only when she would arrive.

"I'd offer you dinner," Cota said. "But I gather you're the type that would rather talk business, and not fuss around with social amenities, am I right?"

"Reason I'm here."

He set the glass down, used the tongs to drop another ice cube into it.

"This is thirty years old," he said. "If you're someone who appreciates a fine single malt, I'd recommend you try it."

"Thanks anyway." She drank little, almost always wine, and never when working. For her, the work had started the moment she'd left the terminal and seen Hicks waiting there.

"I admire the care you take," Cota said. "It speaks well of you. I'm sure you were concerned when I suggested we meet here, at my house. But I'm a public person. I'm occasionally recognized on the street, when I have the rare occasion to be out there. And we couldn't very well meet at a bar or a hotel or wherever these types of discussions are traditionally conducted. Also, I wanted to meet you face-to-face. I didn't want to send just Randall here, for example. I wanted you to see me, know exactly who you were dealing with. I owed you that much."

"I appreciate it."

"So it made more sense to have him meet you at the airport, bring you directly here. And anyway, I expect you did quite a bit of research about me before you boarded that plane in the first place."

"A little."

"Then you know who I am, and what I am. Some of what

you've undoubtedly read is true, and a lot of it—I assure you—isn't, but . . ." He shrugged. "What can you do?"

"I'm here," she said. "That tells you something."

"It does. It does. Say we take a stroll, out into the garden perhaps? Would that make you feel better? I think it would, wouldn't it?"

"Up to you."

He sipped scotch, put the tip of his cane against the floor, and got slowly to his feet, his face showing the effort. Hicks watched him but made no move to help.

"Randall," Cota said, "we'll be taking the air. Amuse yourself." Still carrying the glass, he tipped the cane toward another doorway. "After you."

They went downstairs into an even larger room, more art on the walls, through French doors and into the garden. There were key lights out there now, lining a path, and she could see small statues every few feet, the greenery cut back around them. Flute-playing Pans, satyrs, cherubs, mourning women. There were lights in the fountain, too, giving the water a soft blue glow. In its center was a statue of a muscular naked man, one arm extended, a leg raised behind him as if he were in flight.

The jasmine smell was strong here. A breeze moved the willows, the tips of their branches sweeping the ground.

"I'm guessing our mutual friend didn't tell you much," Cota said. "As I told him very little in turn. It took me quite a bit of effort to find him. A name here, a name there. People who knew people. I considered it quite an accomplishment when I finally established contact with him. But money will open a lot of doors, especially if you're not afraid to spend it. Sit?" He pointed the cane at a marble bench. She shook her head.

"Mind if I do?"

"Go ahead."

He sank down on the bench, grimaced, set the glass beside him. He rested one elbow on the head of his cane, looked up at her. There were trickles of sweat on his face.

"I'm a collector," he said. "As I'm sure you know. You've seen some of what I have here. There's more in my other houses as well. In New York, in Grenada and Brussels. And two warehouses, in Nevada and Arizona. It's a sin how much I've acquired. But it's what motivates me. Wanting things. Our passions keep us young, don't you think?"

"Maybe."

He drank scotch again, the cubes melted and gone.

"About four years ago, I bought some items that were, let's say, highly collectible. Antiquities. They'd been appropriated from a place that was in a state of chaos at the time. No rule of law there, no one to decide what belonged to whom. But I guess one might say, in the strictest sense of the term, these items were stolen."

"Go on."

"Regardless, I saw them as an investment opportunity. If I didn't acquire them, someone else would. Plus, there was a limited window of time on their availability. So I secured the items where they were and eventually, at great personal expense, had them brought here to the States."

She heard a keening moan from the hills behind the house, turned toward it.

"Coyote," he said. "They come around here sometimes, when there's a drought, or a brush fire. Or they're hungry. On occasion a neighborhood dog will get loose, hear that fellow and follow him up into the hills. He thinks it's his long-lost brother, or possibly a mate. Instead he gets killed, and eaten. There's a lesson there, I'm sure."

She said nothing, waited for him to go on.

"As I was saying, I warehoused these antiquities over here, and started searching for a buyer. Sotto voce, of course, because you can hardly trust anyone in this business. But there was so much fuss about these particular items, and their provenance, that I searched in vain for months.

"Unfortunately, along the way there were people I'd dealt with who weren't as circumspect as I. Perhaps they had an ax to grind, felt I'd bested them in some business deal. They took money, I'm sure, for providing the information to authorities. Either way, the end result was that my ownership of these items—questionable as it was—came to the attention of some organizations that would rather they be repatriated to where they'd come from, where, then at least, things were relatively calmer and more secure."

"Iraq," she said.

"The where doesn't matter. My hand was forced. These authorities and I came to an agreement that involved my returning the items—at my own expense. I agreed to assure their transit to a place where they could be handed over to an agent for the government that now claims to be the original owners—though that claim is as questionable as any other. In my view, I had as much right to those artifacts as anyone, considering what I'd spent on them, the risks I'd taken."

"What do you mean?"

"Look at any great museum in the world. What are they filled with? Plunder. It's how we learn about the past, how we keep it alive. These items belong in the hands of people who understand them, value them, who have the resources and the will to protect them. Not leave them at the mercy of whatever temporary, bloody-minded regime happens to come to power.

"Do you know what the Taliban did in Afghanistan, to some of the oldest statuary in the world, priceless treasures that date back more than two thousand years? You've heard of the Buddhas of Bamiyan?"

She shook her head.

"The tallest Buddha figures in the world, one of them a hundred and eighty feet high, carved out of a sandstone cliff. They were destroyed, dynamited, because those who'd come to power decided they were examples of anti-Muslim idolatry. And there were more barbarous acts of the same nature, throughout the entire region. Now, if someone had spirited some of those items away, saved them, protected them, what would be wrong with that?"

"But the ones you spirited away, you now have to give back."

He nodded, took a handkerchief from his shirt pocket and wiped sweat from his forehead.

"And as I said, at my expense, with the one allowance being that there would be no questions asked, and no ridiculous international investigation or specious charges to waste everyone's time. But my name was known, and the presence of these items in my warehouse was known, so I had no choice."

"They were going to let you just return them and walk away? That doesn't sound right."

"There were some extenuating circumstances. If the full story of how I acquired them were to come out, it would cast a certain ambitious government official over there in a very bad light. No doubt, he'd lose the lofty status he's since obtained. This way, it's much quieter. They get their items back and I take the loss—quietly."

"I still don't understand why I'm here."

"Well, the final joke fate played on me in this matter? To fully prove me fortune's fool? During the middle of all these egregious—and expensive—negotiations, the unforeseen happened."

"You got a buyer."

He nodded, leaned on the cane. "Someone I'd dealt with before. Someone I had in mind when I first acquired these objects, but who, at the time, wouldn't go near them, because of the controversy attached."

"And now he thinks you're a motivated seller, so you'll take his price, which is less than you wanted."

"You see it exactly. As you can imagine, it presents a dilemma."

"Because now you have to give them back, and you can't make the deal."

"I've arranged for their transportation, at my own expense, from my warehouse outside Las Vegas to a port in Southern California. That's where they'll be handed over to begin the first leg of their journey back to their supposed homeland."

"And you'd rather they not get there," she said. "Because you'd rather sell them than give them back."

He folded the handkerchief, put it away. "Until that handover, until they're unloaded from my truck at that port, they're still under my control. You're familiar with the term, I'm sure, that some crimes—some robberies, most particularly—are called 'give-ups'?"

She nodded, knowing where this was going, what he wanted, why she was here.

"I would very much like," he said, "during that long, perilous journey across the desert, for someone to rob me."

TWO

In the Jaguar, headed back down the winding streets, she said, "Not very inconspicuous, is it?"

"What?" Hicks said. "The car? Out here, trust me, nobody notices."

"What else do you do for him when you're not driving?"

"A little of everything. But if you're thinking it's one of those sugar-daddy situations, well, I wish. I have to work for a living. I keep a room there I use sometimes, but that's it."

"You have a title?"

"I guess you could call me his head of security."

"He needs one?"

"Doesn't everybody?"

The road grew steep, and he downshifted, took the next turn easily. The road was lined with trees, high fences.

She nodded at the tattoo on his forearm. "Nice work. Where'd you get it?"

"Thanks. This one"—he turned his arm out, the muscles flexing beneath the skin—"was right here in the States. Down in San Pedro, out on the pier. I like yours, too."

He gestured to her left hand, the Chinese character etched on the inside of her wrist, a faint white burn scar across it.

"It's Chinese," she said. "It means—"

"Perseverance. I know. It suits you."

"You don't even know me."

"Just a guess. Where'd you get it?"

"Texas."

"I bet there's a story goes with it."

"There is," she said.

When she didn't go on, he smiled, shook his head. She looked out through the windshield, headlights cutting through the darkness.

"So just what is it you're in charge of securing?" she said.

"You'd be surprised. The house, of course, especially when he has events, exhibitions of his collection, whatever. I do the same at his other places, as needed. Occasionally I have to fly out, handle a situation at one of the warehouses or offices. It keeps me busy."

"You do all that yourself?"

"I have people I use when I need them. A team. Guys I served with."

"I guessed. What branch?"

He looked at her. "Corps all the way. First Battalion, Fifth Marine Regiment. First over the berm, March 20, '03."

"The what?"

"The berm. That's what we called the southern border of Iraq and Kuwait. We'd been waiting for days, going crazy in the heat, so it was a relief to get moving."

"How long were you over there?"

"Two deployments. Rotated out in 2006, then eventually got a job stateside with a private security firm. Next thing I knew I was back over there as an independent contractor. Made a hell of a lot more money that time, though."

The road straightened. Through the trees she could see the lights of the boulevard down there, traffic moving along at a crawl.

"It must have been dangerous," she said.

"The more you learn, the less dangerous it is. And bits of wisdom get passed on, stuff you don't learn in your training, or from a manual."

"Like what?"

They came to a red light. He eased the car to a stop, rested his wrists on the steering wheel.

"Lots of things," he said. "For example, we used to have a saying, 'When the pin is out, Mr. Grenade is not your friend.'"

"Good advice."

"Reason is, guys go to toss a grenade out of a moving vehicle, to break up an ambush, whatever, sometimes they pull the pin, pop the spoon right there in their lap. You need to have both hands out the window when you do that. Otherwise, you hit a bump, drop that baby inside your vehicle, and it's good night, Irene."

The light changed. They made a left, and then they were on a side road that fed onto Sunset. She'd given him the name of a hotel there. At the intersection, he made another left, and they merged into traffic.

"Listen," he said. "I know you just got here, and you're probably tired, jet lag and all. But since we're going to be working together . . ."

"Who said that?"

"Well, since there's a *chance* we'll be working together, can I buy you a drink before you turn in? Someplace quiet?"

"Thanks anyway. Maybe another time."

"You got it. No worries. This it up here on the right?"

"Yes," she said.

He signaled, pulled into the breezeway of the hotel. The glass doors slid open, and a valet came out, a kid in his twenties with the blond good looks of a surfer.

Hicks parked, left the engine running. When they got out, she shook her head at the valet. Hicks got her bag from the trunk, shut the lid.

"I guess we'll be talking," he said. "If you need anything, call."

She'd bought a disposable cell phone before she left New Jersey, had exchanged numbers with him. The one he'd given her would be a burner as well, she knew. Another precaution.

"I will," she said, and took the bag.

"Do I call you Chris, Christine, what?"

"Doesn't matter. Either's fine."

"Well, it was good meeting you." He held out his hand.

She looked at it for an awkward moment, but he didn't draw it back. She took it. His grip was warm and dry.

"You've got a good handshake," he said. "Strong. I like that."

She looked at him, but there was no sarcasm there.

"Get some rest," he said, and got back behind the wheel.

She watched him drive off, the valet hovering a few feet away. When the car was out of sight, she turned to him.

"Can I have that taken to your room?" he said.

"No," she said. "Just get me a cab."

*　*　*

She gave the driver the name of the motel in Culver City where she had a reservation. It was in a residential area, bungalows and small houses, the motel set back from the road.

She checked in, carried her bag to the room. From the front desk operator, she got the number of a local rental agency, called and arranged to have a car delivered in the morning.

She opened her bag atop the bureau but didn't unpack. If she didn't like what she heard tomorrow, she'd leave immediately, catch the next flight east.

She showered and changed, feeling the fatigue now, the displacement of long-distance travel. She was too tired to leave the room, scout around for a place to eat. There was a folder on the desk with menus from local takeout places. She'd order in, rest, sleep. Tomorrow, she'd listen to the rest of what they had to say. And then she'd decide.

Hicks laid out the photos in front of her. They were 8-by-10 color prints of a large statue, a winged bull with a man's head and a square beard. It seemed to be emerging from a wall, half freed from the stone. A piece was broken cleanly off the top, and other spots were cracked and chipped.

"Assyrian," Cota said from across the table. "Seven twenty-one BC."

They were in the big room on the third floor, the French doors closed, a pair of ceiling fans turning slowly in the shadows above. Hicks sat to her left.

"How much does it weigh?" she said.

"Five hundred pounds," Cota said. "Give or take. It's called a *lamassu*. A mythical creature, sort of the Assyrian version of a sphinx. It was built to guard the throne room of Sargon II, in Dar-Sharrukin."

"Where's that?" she said.

"Northern Iraq," Hicks said. "Near Mosul. At least that's what it is now."

"This one will give you a sense of scale," Cota said.

In the next photo, the statue rested on a large wooden pallet, half covered by a canvas tarp. A dark-skinned man in green fatigues stood beside it. The top of the statue was even with his shoulder.

"There's another one like it, much larger, at the University of Chicago," Cota said. "In their Oriental Institute. And a third at the British Museum in London. This one is the smallest of the lot, and has sustained more damage than the others, as you can see. Who knows what might have happened to it eventually, if I hadn't brought it here?"

Hicks took more photos from a tan folder, set them out. There were pictures of the statue from different angles, all taken in the same high-ceilinged warehouse space.

"You take these for potential buyers?" she said.

"For the serious ones," Cota said. "If it got to that stage, yes."

The seventh photo was of a different piece, half the size of the first. A section of wall depicting two robed figures with elaborate headdresses and the same square beards.

"From the same excavation," Cota said.

The last three photos were of the bust of a man's head. Wide staring eyes, curved beard, the neck ending in a jagged edge where it had been broken from a larger statue. There was a wooden ruler on the canvas next to it for scale. The height was a little over seven inches.

"Don't let the size deceive you," Cota said. "That's one of the most valuable pieces that's ever crossed my hands. It's from the Third Dynasty of Ur. 2000 BC."

She looked through the photos again. "I don't know anything about this type of stuff."

"You don't need to. I just wanted you to get a sense of what we're talking about."

"Just these three?"

"That's it," Hicks said.

"These other two could be moved easily enough, but that one . . ." She touched the photo of the winged bull.

"It's actually in three segments," Cota said. "That's how we had it transported over here, by ship. We reassembled it once it arrived, for photographic purposes. It has to be crated and moved as three separate units, though."

"Who's the man in the photo?"

"His name is Hashemi Rafsan. He was my expert in those matters."

"Military?"

"He was," Hicks said. "Iraqi Army, Republican Guard, until he saw us come tear-assing across the desert."

"A pragmatist above all else," Cota said. "He was very useful to me."

"He was my point man over there," Hicks said. "To help decide what was worth the risk, what wasn't. He'd worked at the National Museum in Baghdad before the war."

"He know about all these? What you were bringing over?"

"He did," Hicks said.

"Where is he now?"

"Regrettably, he's no longer with us," Cota said.

"How's that?"

"It's still a dangerous place over there," Hicks said. "Even now."

She lined up the photos in two rows. Hicks sat back, crossed his arms, watching her.

"When is all this supposed to happen?" she said.

"One month," Cota said. "That's the timetable we agreed on. If it's going to take more time, I have to let them know. They won't be happy, though, and I'd like to avoid giving any impression of reluctance. Would four weeks be sufficient time?"

"It might be," she said. "Let it ride for now. Don't tell them any different." She looked at the first picture again. "Five hundred pounds."

"It had to be taken by boat down the Tigris," Cota said. "Then by rail to the port of Umm Qasr. As I said, there was considerable expense involved."

"And I'd guess considerably more if you have to pay the freight all the way back to where you got it."

"One of their stipulations," Cota said. He rested his cane in his lap. "As I said, a dilemma. And an expensive one."

"Your new buyer, how do you get the pieces to him?"

Cota looked at Hicks. "Randall?"

"We haven't worked out all the details yet," Hicks said. "But I think a simple detour works best. The truck carrying the items is supposed to go to Long Beach, where a rep from the Iraqi government will meet it at the port, sign off on the contents, supervise the shipping. However, our real buyer will be waiting at another port with his own ship, a hundred miles away."

"Where?"

"San Diego."

"That's a long haul."

"But the hard part will be over. My thought is we intercept the truck after it leaves the warehouse, somewhere out in the desert. Then we tie up the personnel, drive off with the goods. Once we do the handover to the buyer, it's his problem. Hopefully, by the time anyone figures out what's happened, his ship will have sailed."

"A truck hijacked while returning stolen goods under duress," she says. "Hard coincidence to buy, isn't it?"

"A chance we have to take," Cota said. "My options are limited."

"You could go through with it," she said.

"What do you mean?"

"Give them back."

"I think not." He looked at Hicks, who nodded, got up and left the room.

"How many people traveling with this circus?" she said.

"Five men. But as I said, they're all my employees, or ones I've subcontracted."

"Any of them in on this?" If the answer was yes, she'd be on a plane home tonight.

"They don't need to be," he said. "They're always under strict instructions not to resist if there's an issue. And with the little I pay them, I doubt that interfering with armed bandits will enter into their thinking. It wouldn't be worth it."

"Let's hope they remember that."

"I wouldn't be overly concerned. And having them there is to our advantage. They'll tell their stories afterward, and quite truthfully. The convoy was stopped, the truck taken, and that was that."

She looked at the photos again.

"Should I consider your interest piqued?" he said.

"Lots of logistics."

"That I would leave up to you. Hicks will be at your service. Others, too, if you need them. His associates."

"What's the personnel breakdown on the convoy?"

"A single truck, two cars. One leading, one following. There will be a driver and a guard in both of the cars. But only a driver in the truck."

"Armed?"

"The guards, yes."

"Will they have radios?"

"To communicate between the vehicles? No."

"But cell phones, I'm sure, all of them."

"I would expect so."

"That's a problem."

"Again, I bow to your expertise in those matters."

Hicks came back in carrying a legal-sized manila envelope. He put it on the table, sat back down. On a lower floor a cuckoo clock began to chime. Nine P.M.

"At least five people to be dealt with," she said. "So you'd need a three-person team going in. Four would be better. Easier to manage the variables."

"If that's what you suggest," Cota said.

"How will the truck be packed?" she said. "Lots of padding, I would expect. Crates?"

"Big ones," Hicks said. "With foam rubber padding, and sandbags to keep them from shifting in transit."

"Locks?"

"Nothing special," he said. "Oversized padlock on the rear

door, crossbar, standard for that type of truck. A sledgehammer and a pry bar would do the trick."

"Or we could procure an extra key," Cota said. "Much less effort."

"No," she said. "It has to look like what it is. A robbery. A key says inside job."

"Ah," Cota said.

"Still," she said, "I'm a little surprised. Items like these, shouldn't there be more security involved? Armored car, maybe? More vehicles, at least. This sounds bare bones."

"Randall, would you care to explain?"

She turned to Hicks.

"It's a little different in the antiquities world," he said. "We do this kind of thing all the time. Transporting, I mean. The object is to keep it as low profile as you can. The more security you have, the more people know you're moving something valuable. Instead, you do it simple and quick, attract as little attention as possible."

"These things will be insured, I'm guessing?"

"Of course," Cota said.

"Will the insurance company want to send someone along for the ride, keep an eye out?"

"They haven't before," Cota said. "No reason to think they'd insist upon it this time. If they did, they'd have notified me already."

She nodded at the envelope. "What's that?"

"I thought," Cota said, "since you came all the way out here at your own expense, the least I could do was reimburse you. Whether we move forward, or you walk out of here tonight and we never meet again. Either way, I want you to keep that."

He slid the envelope closer to her.

"How much is in there?" she said.

"Five thousand," Cota said. "Cash, of course. Just a gesture."

"No thanks," she said. She slid it back toward him. "If I decide to help you out, then we'll talk about money. And it'll be a lot more than five thousand."

"Of course," Cota said. "But I insist you take that in the meantime, as a gesture of good faith."

"She doesn't want any obligations," Hicks said. "She wants to be able to walk away without any strings attached, any debts." He looked at her. "Am I right?"

"Something like that."

Cota sat back. "As you wish."

"As long as we're talking money," she said, "how much are these things worth?"

"On the open market," Cota said, "who knows? On one level, they're priceless. Let's just say what I'm taking for them is quite a bit less than their actual value, which is considerable."

"As is the risk."

"Fair enough. When you say it might require a four-person team, you're including yourself?"

"Yes."

"Then here would be my proposition. Two hundred thousand cash to you, a hundred thousand to whoever you bring in. Half when they sign on, half when it's done. Would you consider that equitable?"

"Four might not do it," she said. "I wouldn't know until I got into it. It might take five."

"Then the fifth man—or woman—comes out of the same pie.

Two hundred thousand to you, seventy-five to each of your people—or however you want to divide it up. Five hundred thousand total. And don't forget, Hicks will be available to help as well, as needed. Equipment, logistics, tactics, whatever. In fact, the one thing I will insist upon is that he go along on this 'mission,' so to speak."

"If it happens."

"Indeed, if. And his end isn't part of the five hundred. I pay him myself. The rest is yours, to divide as you see fit. And as I said, half now, half when it's done."

She slid the pictures back into the folder. "I'll take these with me."

"If you think that's wise," Cota said.

"I'll also need to look at maps, specs on the truck, the warehouse, personnel. Everything you can give me."

"I can get you all that," Hicks said.

"Good." She closed the folder, stood.

"I'll walk you out," Hicks said. "I'm headed back to my own place."

"Where's that?"

"Venice. I have a condo by the beach there."

"All right," she said. Then to Cota, "I'm going to look all this over, along with whatever else Hicks gives me. He can deal with me directly."

"How will I know what you've decided?" Cota said.

"If I'm in," she said, "you'll get a phone call."

"And if I don't, you're not," he said. "Because you will have already left Los Angeles."

"That's right."

"And I'll be left to worry what you might do with the knowledge you already have."

"I don't work like that," she said.

He looked at the envelope with the money, then back at her.

"No," he said. "I believe you don't."

THREE

The hotel on Sunset had an outdoor bar on the second floor, next to a swimming pool. Tiki torches threw shadows on the patio, and light shimmer reflected from the water. The deck looked out on dark hills dotted with the lights of houses. She wondered which one was Cota's.

They sat at a table near the railing, Crissa with a glass of red wine, Hicks on his second scotch. A citronella candle flickered between them. He'd repeated his invitation when they were leaving the house, and this time she'd accepted, suggested here. They'd come in separate cars, and she'd met him at the bar.

"So," he said. "What do you think about what you've heard so far?"

She looked around. The tables near them were empty. Most of the drinkers were at the inside bar, clustered around a large-screen TV showing a baseball game.

"I'll take a look at what you get me," she said. "Then maybe we can figure out a way to do it. Or not. How long have you worked for him?"

"Three years in September. He hired me away from the outfit I'd been working with. It was too good a deal to turn down. A lot safer, too."

"He ever do anything like this before?"

"Robbing himself? No, this is a one-off. Like he said, he ended up in a jam, and this was the plan he came up with to get himself out. You have to give him credit for even thinking of it. After all, it's a victimless crime, isn't it?"

"Maybe not. It depends on how things play out."

"You're right. But you can't work out every possibility in advance, can you? You just plan the best you can, and improvise if things start going south."

"That's true. But you can always plan better."

He sat back, laced his fingers behind his head. "I'm guessing you know all about that. But I gotta say, I never expected to find a woman like you in this line of work."

"Like me?"

"That didn't come out right. I mean, someone like you putting this kind of thing together, running a team."

She didn't respond, drank wine, waiting to see where he'd take it.

"Oh, hell, forget I said it. I'm feeling the liquor, I guess. That's why you came along anyway, right?"

She put her glass down. "What do you mean?"

"Get a few drinks in me, hope I'll run off at the mouth, tell you something you don't know. It wasn't my charm got us up here, was it?"

"It was your idea."

"You're all business. I appreciate that."

"Not always." Surprised she'd said it, wondering why she had.

"And I'm guessing you're not even staying in this hotel, are you?"

"Why do you say that?"

"Because you wouldn't have brought me here if you were. You keep your distance. That's smart."

A breeze came in from the hills, the scent of eucalyptus. The torches fluttered.

"Tell me more about your employer," she said.

"How much do you know?"

"Mostly what's common knowledge. Where's he from originally? I've read different versions."

"Czechoslovakia. His family fled during the war. They moved around a lot, but I think he grew up mostly in England. Worked at a couple newspapers there, made his way up the ladder. Ended up buying the papers, then a publishing house."

"Where did his money come from?"

"He earned it, I guess. Eventually he sold off the properties he owned in England, moved to the States, started doing the same thing here."

"From what I read, mostly what he did was buy companies and put them out of business, after skimming bonuses for himself."

"He knows when to drop a losing proposition, is all. He's smart that way. If he gets stuck in a place he doesn't like, gets dealt a bad hand, whatever, he figures a way out of it."

"They used to call that a bust-out," she said.

"What?"

"A mob thing, back in the day. They'd buy into a legitimate business, one that was struggling, needed some cash. They'd borrow money with the business as collateral, sell off all its assets, then shut it down, leave someone else holding the bill. Or torch it for the insurance money."

He scratched his elbow. "I wouldn't know anything about that. I admire him, though. He knows what he wants, and he goes out and gets it. He didn't let the world fuck him over. He started out with nothing, and look where he is now."

"Living alone in a house filled with millions of dollars in art he doesn't even notice anymore?"

"It's his art, and that's what counts. He may not notice it, but trust me, if some of it went missing, he'd do whatever he had to do to get it back. Just on principle."

"Not my line," she said. "He's got nothing to worry about."

The waitress came over. She was in her twenties, blue-eyed and blond, in tight black slacks and a white blouse with a man's tie. Hicks gave her a smile, pointed to their almost-empty glasses. "I think we'll do another, honey. Thank you." She smiled back, took them to the bar.

"How about you?" Crissa said. "Where are you from originally?"

"Virginia. Town called Bluefield. Got out of there soon as I could, though. Two semesters of community college, then I joined the Corps. Still not sure why. Just my luck, a year later, we were in the middle of two wars. All that shit happened fast."

"What was your rank?"

"When I left? Staff sergeant. Over there, though, what you got was battlefield commissions. Those first couple years were crazy. We were in Fallujah, and later on, Anbar Province. Saw some wild shit. Lost some good men."

"But you went back."

"Weren't a whole lot of opportunities around when I left the Corps. Economy was still fucked, and there wasn't much I knew how to do. Couldn't see getting a job in some factory, knocking up a local girl, living happily ever after and all that."

"Was there one?"

"A what?"

"A local girl." Wanting to take back the question now, too late. Not sure why she'd asked it.

He sat back, cocked his head, squinted at her slightly. "If there was, I probably wouldn't have joined the Corps. Is this where we get into the personal stuff? If so, it's going to be your turn next."

She shook her head. "Sorry. None of my business. Just curious."

He shrugged. "That's fine. I don't mind."

The waitress brought their drinks. As she walked away, she let her fingers trail lightly over his shoulder.

When she was out of earshot, Crissa said, "You should come here more often. You could probably drink for free."

"This town's crazy like that. Women all over the place. I still can't get used to it. It's a long way from Bluefield."

"I'm sure it is. What else can you tell me about Cota?" Wanting to steer it back to business, regretting the detour she'd let it take.

"Like what?"

"He have family here? I know he was married at one point."

"Divorced a long time ago. They had one kid, a son. He was killed in a car accident when he was seventeen. I don't think Emile ever got over that. That's what ended the marriage, I'd guess. Most people don't understand. Tragedies like that—ones that come out of the blue and don't make any sense—they don't bring families closer together, they blow them apart."

"You sound like you're speaking from experience."

He grinned. "You keep going, don't you? Always digging."

"Sorry."

"That's all right. Now what about you? Where are you from?"

"The South."

"And that's all you're going to tell me, isn't it?"

"Does it matter where I'm from?" She felt a smile coming, lifted her glass to drink.

"I guess not. Anybody back home ever call you Red?"

Her smile faded. She set the glass back down. "Someone used to. A long time ago."

"Ah."

A cry rose up from the crowd inside.

"I think it's time to call it a night," she said. She slid the glass away. "Lots to do tomorrow."

"You're not going to finish that?"

"I'm good."

"Sorry," he said. "None of my business what you do. I need to remember that."

He looked down at his drink. She saw the disappointment in his face, wondered what it was he'd been hoping for. Better not to alienate him, to keep things easy between them for now.

"So what do I call you?" she asked.

He looked up. "What?"

"What do you prefer? Randy, Randall, what?"

"Randy," he said. "Randy's fine."

She stood. "Well, Randy. Thanks for the drink." She got her leather jacket from the back of the chair.

"Maybe we can do this again sometime," he said.

"Maybe."

"I won't walk you out. You want to leave first anyway, right, keep that distance? I'll stay here, have another drink."

"Be careful driving. We'll talk tomorrow."

At the patio door, she looked back. The waitress had returned, was standing by the table, one hip against it. He was smiling up at her. He looked younger from the distance.

He caught her watching, looked at her, the waitress still talking. She turned and went through the door.

Downstairs in the breezeway, she gave the valet her ticket, watched the traffic go by on Sunset, breathed in the cool night air. Loud music came from a bar across the street. A crescent moon hung over the dark hills to the east.

Tomorrow she'd contact Sladden, tell him she was in. He'd be due a finder's fee, then a percentage of her final take if all went well. There would be maps for her to look at, more photos, more details to consider. Then she would start making calls.

FOUR

"Here's how it's going to work," she said.

They were at the table in the upstairs room, papers and photos spread out in front of them. Hicks had dark circles under his eyes, was drinking water from a plastic bottle.

"Late night?" she said.

"Little dehydrated, is all."

"You make it to Venice?"

He smiled. "Not quite."

Cota put on reading glasses, looked at the map she'd set in front of him, said, "Go ahead."

She tapped the map with the eraser end of a pencil.

"From what you've told me, the truck will leave your warehouse in the late afternoon. Maybe three o'clock before it's ready to roll, correct?"

"By the time it's loaded and inspected, yes."

"When they leave, they'll head south, then west onto I-15. It's the most direct route. That takes them through some pretty barren patches of desert, especially between here"—she tapped the map—"and here." She tapped it again. "That's where we'll do it."

"Where exactly?" Hicks said. "That's a long stretch of road."

"I'll decide after I've been out there, had a look. Now, the later the truck gets under way, the better for us. I'd like to do this with dusk coming on. That way when we're pulling out of there it'll be night. That also means less chance the truck will be spotted after we drive it away."

"Good thinking," Hicks said.

"Somewhere on that stretch of I 15, we'll stop the convoy," she said. "Some sort of diversion we'll work out later. When I've had a look at the terrain, I'll pick a likely place. We'll be there already, hidden, waiting. I'll have three of my own people with me, and Hicks." She looked at him. "Might be good to have one of your guys there as well, just in case."

"What do you see me doing?"

"Personnel control. We need to get them locked down fast. As soon as the convoy stops, we'll go in heavy, get everyone out of those vehicles and secured before they even know what's happening. Some scary weaponry might help, M-16s, whatever. Something they'll respect. I'll leave that to you."

"Got it," he said.

"What about the cell phone issue?" Cota said.

"I have some ideas on that," she said. "We can talk about them later."

"All right." Hicks leaned closer to the map. "Go on."

"One of my people will be a driver," she said. "He'll take the truck. We don't want to travel too far in a stolen rig, so we'll stash a second one somewhere nearby, transfer the items into it. Will there be enough gear in the truck to do that? Forklifts, handcarts, whatever?"

"There will," Cota said. "They'd have to off-load it when it got to the port anyway, so any necessary equipment will already be on the truck."

"It has a hydraulic tailgate lift," Hicks said. "And there's a heavy-duty forklift inside to move the pallets and crates. Transferring these types of items isn't as difficult as it sounds. I've done it. You hook the pallet, ride the lift down, then reverse the procedure at the other truck. A one-man job, but quicker with two."

"That equipment enough to handle this *lamassu*?"

"No sweat."

She looked at Cota. "Can you get us a second truck without too many people knowing about it? It should be as much like the first one as possible. The closer the better."

"I can do that."

"This right there," Hicks slid a photo toward her, "is the one we're using. On the back are all the specs if you need them, fuel capacity, mileage, displacement, weight limit, everything."

"Good." It was a medium-sized moving van, but with two tires on each side in the rear. It was painted white, with no lettering, would be inconspicuous on any interstate.

"We gather the five people—and hopefully it is only five— disarm the guards and flexcuff everybody," she said. "Get them out of our way, and all in one place so they're easily managed. Can you get some netting or tarp, desert camo colors?"

"Probably," Hicks said. "Why?"

"We're taking the truck with us, but we'll be leaving the two cars. When we're done, we get them off the road, camouflage them as best we can. It might buy us some time."

She traced the eraser along the map. "Until I get out there, I won't know for sure, but I'm guessing this highway, given where it is, may not be that well traveled, but it won't be deserted either. There'll be traffic on and off, so we need to get this whole thing wrapped up fast. Five minutes, tops."

"Not much time," Hicks said.

"We plan it right, that's all we'll need," she said.

"And what if someone comes along during those five minutes?" Cota said.

"We'll have lookouts to warn us. If someone does stop, we'll just have to improvise." She looked at Hicks.

"I got it," he said. "We'll work it out."

"This thing goes fast, or it doesn't go at all," she said. "Once we get our team assembled, we need to practice, drill. Another reason we need the second truck. It should have the same tailgate lift, same weight specs, same equipment inside."

"Shouldn't be a problem," Hicks said.

"We'll work with that. Get a feel for the equipment, learn our way around it. Once we know what we're doing, five minutes should be a comfortable amount of time."

"What kind of distance are we talking about here?" Hicks said.

She turned the map around to face him, slid it closer.

"The original route, from outside Vegas to the port at Long Beach, is about three hundred miles. But the truck isn't going to make it to Long Beach. In fact, it won't even make it to the Nevada line."

"How so?"

"That's where the second truck comes in. When we're done practicing on it, we'll stow it somewhere not far from where we'll stop the convoy. We can use those camo nets on it as well, so it won't be spotted from the air. Might be good to have something painted on its side, too, moving company, whatever." She looked at Cota. "Do we have to worry about GPS, on the items or the truck?"

"No. I shouldn't think so."

She turned to Hicks again. "That makes it easier. When we grab the truck, we drive it to where the other one's waiting, transfer all the pieces, camo the old truck and leave it behind."

"Smart," Hicks said. "I hadn't considered that."

"The second truck will be clean, so there's no reason anyone should stop it along the way. My driver takes it to where the buyer's waiting, parks it and walks away. Then our part's done. The rest is someone else's problem."

"And you think this will work?" Cota said. "The way you've laid it out? In the time frame we have?"

She met his eyes. "I wouldn't be here if I didn't."

"No offense intended."

She folded the map. "I'll start gathering my people." She looked at Hicks. "You should find your second man, too."

"I will. No worries."

"Tomorrow I'm going to go out and have a look at possible sites," she said. "I'll let you know what I find."

"You'll have expenses," Cota said.

"I will. And I'll take that five thousand now."

"I'll get it," Hicks said, and left the room. She put the map and photos back in the folder.

Cota took off his glasses. "You work fast."

"Isn't that why you hired me?"

"It feels like, just a few days ago, this was only a wild idea. And now it seems a possibility."

"It's not too late to back out."

He looked at the folder, shook his head. "In for a penny. If I thought there was another solution, I'd gladly take it. But the way you set this out . . . well, it doesn't seem so wild after all."

"There's the issue of my down payment. The hundred thousand."

"Of course, I'll see to it right away."

"Wait until I get out there, have a look. If for some reason I decide it can't be done, then we'll talk."

Hicks came back into the room with the same manila envelope she'd seen before. He set it in front of her. "Want to count it?"

"I will. Later."

He smiled, sat back down.

To Cota, she said, "I'll eventually need more, for expenses. If so, you'll have to wire it to me wherever I am."

"Of course."

"And as soon as my people are signed on, they'll need their front-end money."

"I'll see to that as well."

"And expenses are separate. They don't come out of the two hundred you'll owe me."

"I never thought otherwise."

"You'll want to be careful now," she said. "So going forward I'll deal only with Hicks. There's no reason for me to come back here."

"Wise," Cota said. "Now shall we have a drink, to seal it?"

"Sounds good to me," Hicks said.

She looked at him, then back at Cota. Again, it was better to go along. She'd wipe down the glass when she was done. They were in it together now, the work ahead of them.

"Sure," she said. "One drink."

"Capital," Cota said. "Randall, would you find Katya, have her bring the rest of that Macallan? There should be enough left for the three of us."

When he was gone, Cota said, "I feel younger than I have in years."

"Why's that?"

"I'm not quite sure. An excitement that things have been set in motion? That I'm undertaking a bold move in the face of adversity?"

"I mostly look at it as work," she said.

"Very practical. Pragmatic. I like that. It gives me confidence that I've made the right decision."

Katya came into the room carrying the drinks tray, Hicks behind her. She looked at Crissa, then away, set the bottle, ice bowl, and glasses on the table.

"We'll pour," Cota said. "Thank you, Katya. You can go, but find me later, will you? There might be something I need."

He watched her leave the room, then opened the bottle, splashed an inch of scotch into each glass, his hand trembling slightly. He set the bottle back down.

"Neat this time, I think," he said. "To unite us in our mutual undertaking."

He raised his glass.

"To work," he said. He looked at her. "And commensurate reward."

She touched her glass to his, waited for Hicks to lean forward with his own. They clinked glasses, sat back. She drank, felt the liquor go down smooth and warm.

Four weeks, she thought. The time would go fast. But she felt no anxiety now, no uncertainty. She was doing what she knew how to do. She was working.

Hicks sat in the darkened room, sipping scotch, watching the dying fire. Next to him, Cota sat with the cane across his lap. The bottle of Macallan stood empty on the table.

Wood cracked and sparked in the fireplace.

"Your silence is conspicuous, Randall."

"I'm just relaxing. Thinking."

"You've got a lot on your mind, I know." Cota drained his glass, set it beside the bottle. "I don't begrudge you sharing the luxuries of my life. But I do occasionally demand some services in return. Difficult as they may sometimes be."

Hicks didn't answer, looked at the fire.

"That other situation you've been avoiding," Cota said. "It will just get worse the longer you wait. You know that as well as I do."

Hicks drank scotch. "I do."

"He's a danger to you, he's a danger to us. And now he's a danger to this enterprise. It's distasteful to you, I know. You once considered him a friend."

"I still do."

"Then you're naïve. The things he's done, are they the behavior of a friend? He could put us all in prison for a very long time. And he might do it yet, just out of spite. He's angry, and not thinking clearly. That makes him dangerous."

"I know. I'll take care of it."

"When?"

"Soon." He finished his drink.

"I believe you," Cota said. "But I would be very disappointed if my faith was unfounded."

Hicks gripped his glass. "What we're talking about. It's not so easy."

"I never thought it was. But we all must sometimes do things that feel alien to our nature. It's the human condition. Nevertheless, they must be done."

"I said I'll take care of it."

"You feel betrayed by him, I know," Cota said. "You expected better. Perhaps you blame yourself as well for how things turned out. But bitter disappointment is the tissue that binds all of us together, Randall. The sooner we understand that, the sooner we're at peace with the world."

Hicks nodded, looked into the fire. Then he lifted his glass and threw it into the flames.

FIVE

After she signed in, she took a table near the far wall, under the big window, facing the security door he would come through. The other visitors were all women—mostly black or Hispanic—with small children in tow. She made the trip to Texas at least four times a year, and it was always the same in here. Quiet conversations, crying babies. Every once in a while, one of the inmates would look over at her, his eyes lingering. She ignored them.

There were two guards at the visiting-room entrance checking IDs, two more milling around the room, a man and a woman. Central air-conditioning hummed from a vent, but it was still hot in here, sunlight coming through the window above her, illuminating dust motes in the air. There were scuff marks on the black-and-white checkerboard floor. Cameras watched from the four corners of the ceiling.

The security door buzzed, a guard pushed it open from inside, and Wayne came through. He blinked in the sunlight for a moment, saw her and smiled.

She didn't get up. Prison rules allowed physical contact twice during a visit, fifteen seconds at the beginning, another fifteen at the end. But Wayne would never hug her, touch her. He'd said it made it too hard to leave her at visit's end, go back to his cell.

"Hey, darling," he said.

His hair was grayer, his face more gaunt than the last time she'd seen him. His prison blues seemed to hang loose around him. He sat across from her, on a bench bolted to the floor.

"How's it going, handsome?" she said.

He grinned, that lopsided smile that always made something pull inside her. Without thinking, she took his left hand in her right, squeezed. She could see the tattoo on his wrist, the mirror image of her own. He didn't pull away, squeezed back.

"You're looking fine," he said.

"You, too," she said. "How's your back?"

"Better. Coming along. I stretch, that helps." He pointed to her hair. "I'm starting to get used to that. I like it."

The day before, she'd cut her hair short, dyed it black to match the picture on her Texas driver's license. It gave her name as Shana Patrick, with an Austin address. A copy of the license was on file with the unit's approved visitors list. She had to show the original each time she visited.

"Keeping up appearances," she said.

"And looking good while you're doing it. Other cons in here get jealous when you visit. Wonder how an old man like me knows a sweet young thing like you."

"Not so young. And you're not so old."

"Old enough. Too old for you."

"You say that every time. You know I don't like to hear it."

"But it's true. Maybe that's why you don't like it."

"Hands," the female guard said.

Crissa let go, sat back. "You lose a little weight?"

"Me? Nah. All the carbs they feed us in here, I'm surprised I'm not as big as a house."

"You look like you did."

"I'm fine. You been down to Two Rivers?"

That was the town where her daughter, Maddie, lived. She'd turned thirteen earlier that year, was being raised by Crissa's cousin Leah and her husband, Earl. Crissa sent them money every month from a Costa Rican account. Maddie was less than a year old when Crissa had left her with Leah, the only mother the girl had ever known. At nineteen, Crissa was already on the run, in no position to raise a child. And Beaumont, Maddie's father, was long gone as well. In prison now, Crissa guessed. Or dead.

The last time she'd seen Maddie had been four years ago. Crissa had driven down to meet with Leah, had followed her to a neighborhood playground. She'd sat in her rental car, watched Maddie racing around, laughing, Leah watching over her. It had broken her heart.

"Not this time," she said. "This is just a side trip. I'm working."

"Not in Texas, I hope."

She waited for the guard to move away. "No. West Coast."

"So soon?"

The last work she'd done had been in Detroit over a year ago. The take-home had been solid, but there'd been too many bodies left behind. And now the money was running low again.

"I have expenses," she said.

"I'm sure you do. But it makes me worry, knowing you're out there chasing something down."

"Don't. I'll be fine. I had a good teacher."

Wayne had brought her into the Game. Eighteen years older, he'd taken her away from a life of petty crime, shown her how to live. He put crews together, did work across the country. She became part of that world, all the time watching him carefully, learning all she could.

She'd been sick with the flu when it had all gone to hell. He and two other men had robbed a jewelry wholesaler in Houston, a give-up by the owner, who planned to split the take with them and collect the insurance. But a clerk who wasn't in on it had pulled a gun, opened fire. Wayne had ended up with a bullet in his shoulder, and a ten-to-fifteen-year sentence for armed robbery and conspiracy.

Another member of that crew, a pro named Larry Black, had worked the Detroit job with her. He'd been one of the bodies left behind there, shot in the back while the two of them ran from a split gone wrong.

Wayne put his elbows on the table, leaned in closer. "You have a crew yet?"

She looked around, saw the female guard was feeding change into one of the vending machines across the room. Her partner was at the sign-in window, talking to the woman clerk behind the bulletproof glass.

"Not yet," Crissa said. "Putting it together now."

"You running the show?"

"You surprised?"

"Not at all. Just asking. What's the exposure?"

"If it goes right, not much."

"What kind of take-home?"

"Good, but a flat fee. Half up front, half afterward."

He frowned.

"No way around it," she said. "The items in question, I wouldn't know what to do with anyway. So it's work for hire. I do the job and it's over. I don't have to worry about moving anything afterward. All I have to do is plan the work—"

"And work the plan. Yeah, I remember saying that."

"More than once."

"Lot of good it did me."

"I've thought this through. It can work. And with minimal fallout."

He raised an eyebrow. "A give up?"

She nodded. "Mobile. I haven't worked out all the logistics yet."

"Give-ups can go bad, too. Look at me."

"I know. But this is a long way from knocking over check-cashing joints. Or smash-and-grabbing jewelry stores."

He sat back, folded his arms.

"I'm sorry," she said. "That's not how I meant it."

He shrugged. "You're out there. I'm in here. What's it matter what I think?"

"Don't be like that."

"Like what?"

"I want your blessing, you know that. I'm all alone out there. I need to know you're on my side, even when we're apart. I need that."

She felt the distance growing between them. Shut up, she told herself. Don't ruin the little time you have. She moved to touch his hand again, stopped herself.

He watched her for a moment, his face softening. He leaned forward again.

"I'm always on your side, Red. But like I said, I worry. I just wish you'd come talked to me first, before you signed on."

"There wasn't time. And like I said, it's just me out there now. I need to make my own decisions."

"I know."

"Someday I'll get you out of here, get us set up someplace. Together. And that's going to take money. A lot of it."

"Better off spending it on yourself, starting a new life."

"I am."

"One without me."

"I didn't come all the way here to listen to this."

"I'm serious."

"I know. But I'm not ready to start thinking like that yet."

"You will be before long. And sooner's better than later."

She felt a stinging in her eyes, chewed her lip. Trying to find the words.

"You know I'm right," he said.

"You don't know how tough this is for me."

"I do. And you shouldn't have to live like that."

"I feel . . ." But the words were gone. She looked away, then back at him, feeling the wetness in her eyes. "It's like I've got a big empty space here." She touched her chest. "I have a lot to give, and no one to give it to. I need you. None of this makes any sense without you."

He sat back, met her eyes. "Way I look at it, you deserve better."

"You sound like you've giving up hope. I haven't. Not yet. Not ever."

The female guard was watching them. Don't cry, she told herself. Not in here. Don't let these bastards see it.

"If you're trying to cut me loose," she said, "just say it."

"I'm just thinking about what's best for both of us."

"So am I."

"Someday, you know, you're going to have to make a choice."

"Four minutes," the guard said.

Crissa inhaled, let it out slow, centering herself. They'd have to leave it this way for now. Again.

"How are you on money?" she said. "I can put more into your account."

He shook his head. "Plenty in there still. I don't buy much, and there's not much I need. Things are simpler in here, one good thing about it. Keeps your priorities straight."

"Two minutes," the guard said.

"I need to get on the road," Crissa said. "I've got a flight out of San Antone tonight."

"You headed home?"

"Not yet. I have to make a couple stops. People I need to see."

"Anyone I know?"

"Maybe."

"Time," the guard said.

Crissa rose. He looked up at her, then stood.

"Thanks for coming," he said. "But I wish . . ."

She put her arms around him, pulled him close, felt his warmth. He stiffened, tried to draw back, but she held him tighter. He relaxed then, didn't fight it, put his arms around her waist, held her.

"Boudreaux," the male guard said. "Door!"

She felt him start to pull away, gave him a final squeeze, let him go.

He put a hand to her face, thumbed a tear from her eye. "Take care of yourself, Red."

"I love you."

He looked into her eyes, winked, then he was turning away, the guard watching him.

He crossed the room, stood at attention at the closed security door. She looked at his back until the door buzzed open and the guard on the other side waved him through.

He turned at the last minute. His lips formed a kiss, then that smile crossed his face again, and he was gone. The door closed behind him with a solid thump, a snap as the lock engaged.

She stood that way for a moment, looking at the closed door. Then she put on her sunglasses, walked back out into the heat of the day.

SIX

There were lights on in the camper, so Hicks went around it as quietly as he could, walked up the tree-lined driveway in the dark. Winged seedpods crunched under his feet. The camper's hood and windshield were covered with them. It hadn't gone anywhere in a while, if it even ran anymore. A heavy-duty extension cord stretched from a back window, across the lawn to an external outlet on the side of the house. He stepped over it.

Sharon would be waiting for him. He'd called as soon as he'd gotten into Sacramento, hoping that no one answered, that she wouldn't be there. When he'd heard her voice, he had to stop himself from hanging up, turning around and going back to L.A.

He went around to the bare backyard, where a floodlight was mounted over the doorless, half-screened porch. Stiff from the ride, he rotated his neck to get out the kinks, then went up the porch steps, knocked on the kitchen door. Inside, a small dog began to bark.

He looked around. Planks were cracked and missing in the porch floor; what screening there was had rips in half a dozen places. All the money Greggs had brought in back then, and he'd spent none of it here.

He heard her talking to the dog, trying to calm it. Then the door opened and she was smiling at the sight of him.

"How you doing, Sharon?"

The dog, some sort of poodle mix, ran past her and out onto the porch. It circled his legs, barking, snapping its jaws.

"Down, Snowflake," she said. "Down, girl. It's all right."

"You got a killer there."

"Snowflake wouldn't hurt anyone. She just likes to kick up a fuss. Come on in."

He followed her into the kitchen. She closed the door behind them, leaving the dog on the porch. It scratched at the door, barked.

"She'll calm down after a couple minutes. Then I'll let her back in. Sorry about that."

"That's okay. Sorry I got here so late."

The kitchen was old but clean. Peeling linoleum on the floor, an old refrigerator and gas stove. She was barefoot, wore a bathrobe over jeans and a T-shirt, was thinner than he'd last seen her. Her hair was washed-out brown, tied in back. She looked tired.

"I didn't hear you drive up," she said.

"I parked down the block. I didn't want Arlen to know I was here. Wanted to talk to you first."

"Let me get you something to drink, then. Tea? A beer? I think there's some left in here."

"I can't stay long. I just want to talk to Arlen, then I have to get on the road. I'm headed back to L.A. tonight."

"Let's sit, then, at least." The table was Formica and aluminum tubing, at least thirty years old. He waited for her to sit, then drew out a chair for himself. She pushed a loose strand of hair from her eyes.

"I told him you were on your way," she said. "Maybe he'll listen to you. I've given up."

"He stay out there all the time?"

"Hasn't been in the house in weeks. I bring him his food out there, groceries when he needs them. Beer mostly. I asked him to go back to that VA doctor, but that just sets him off. God knows what he does out there all day."

"He ever talk to you about what's going on, what he's thinking?"

"He says he feels safer out there. It's a smaller space, he can 'control the perimeter' better, whatever that means. I don't know what to say when he starts talking like that. I just get upset."

"Anyone else ever come by, talk to him?"

"No. The home health aide visited once, but he wouldn't let her in. He doesn't want to see anyone, talk to anyone. I wish there was something I could do."

"There isn't," he said. "Not at this point. You've been taking good care of him, as far as he'll let you. That's all you can do."

"Maybe. But it just isn't right, living like this. What kind of a marriage is this?"

"I'm sorry. It must be rough on you."

She got up. "I think I'm going to have some of that tea. Sure you don't want any?"

"I'm good," he said. The dog had stopped barking.

She went to the stove, filled a kettle with water and set it on the burner, got the flame going beneath it.

"How many years have you known him, Randy?"

"Long time."

"Longer than we've been married."

"I expect so."

"Was he ever like this before?"

"No, but this isn't the first time I've seen this kind of thing. Guys coming back from active duty, guys who saw combat. They like small spaces, quiet, environments they can control. It's not that unusual."

"Not unusual? We're supposed to be husband and wife, and he lives in a camper parked in the driveway. I'm surprised code enforcement hasn't been out here yet."

She got a mug down from the shelf, a tea bag from a ceramic canister on the counter.

"He's up until all hours of the night," she said. "I see the lights on, hear the TV going. He sleeps mostly in the daytime. Maybe he feels safer then."

"He ever seem . . . I'm not sure how to put this."

"What?" she said.

"Like he'd hurt himself? Do something like that?"

She set a hip against the counter. "I don't think so. I mean, who knows for sure? But he never talks about it, if that's what you mean. He's never threatened it."

"That's good."

The kettle began to whistle. She turned off the flame, poured water into the mug, watched the steam rising up. "I don't know what to do. I really don't."

"I'll talk to him," he said. "But I don't know that it'll do any good."

"You're his oldest friend, Randy. You two went through a lot together. If he'll listen to anybody, it'd be you."

She spooned sugar into the tea, stirred it, sat back down.

"He say anything to you about what's bothering him?" he said. "I mean lately?"

She blew on the tea, shook her head. "Nothing new. It just seems like he's mad at the world. It's the 'effing' this and the 'effing' that. The VA and the politicians and the NSA. And something about drones that doesn't make any sense at all. It's always the same."

He crossed his legs, adjusted his right boot, looked down the short hallway into the living room. It was dark there except for the light of a TV.

"Anybody else here?" he said.

"What do you mean?"

"Anybody. Is there anyone else that's been around here, knows what's going on?" He tilted his head toward the driveway.

"No. He won't see anybody, won't talk to anybody. His sister called once, from North Carolina, but he wouldn't talk to her. Not that I blame him. She has her own problems."

He exhaled, looked around, heard a clock ticking somewhere, voices from the television.

"Well," he said. "I guess there's no sense putting it off."

"He has a cell phone out there. When I need to, I call him from the house phone. You want me to do that?"

"No." He stood. "Don't bother. I have the number. I'll call him when I'm outside."

"He might not say it, but he'll be happy to see you, I bet. He always talks about you."

"What does he say?"

"Just what a great marine you were. That you saved his life in Fallujah. He's always telling that story. Is it true?"

"Some of it. But he exaggerates. We were all in the same boat over there. Just doing our jobs."

"Sometimes it seems like you're the only person in the world he isn't mad at."

"We'll see about that, I guess." He started for the door.

She touched his arm. "Will you come back after you talk to him? Tell me what he said?"

"I will."

He opened the door and the dog rushed in, began to bark at his heels again. Sharon called "Snowflake!" and he eased the dog aside with the edge of his boot, stepped out onto the porch, shut the door. Moths swirled in the floodlight.

As he started down the driveway, he took out his cell, dialed Greggs's number. He answered at the first ring, said, "Where the fuck are you?"

"In your driveway, jagoff. Where do you think?"

"I knew someone was out there. I could hear that goddamn dog."

"You gonna leave me standing around out here, or invite me in?"

"Came all this way, I guess I can give you a minute. It's open."

He went up the frame steps, knocked on the door, stood to the side as a precaution.

"I said it's open."

Inside, the air smelled of stale cigarette smoke and sweat. Greggs sat on an orange daybed, crutches leaning against the wall beside him. He held a .45 automatic in his right hand, pointed at Hicks's chest. The hammer was back.

Hicks raised his hands. "Careful with that."

"Where's your car? I didn't hear it."

"It's down the street."

"Why?"

"I didn't want to disturb Sharon, in case she was sleeping. If she was, I would have turned around, come back tomorrow."

"That your story?"

"It is."

Empty Olympia cans on every flat surface, cigarette butts on the floor. Greggs's prosthetic leg, all gleaming metal and white plastic, was on the table in the breakfast nook, a Nike sneaker on the foot piece. Greggs wore a stained white T-shirt and knee-length camouflage cargo shorts, the left leg loose and empty. On his right foot was the other Nike. He was unshaven, his hair long and dirty.

"Make me nervous," Greggs said. "Sneaking up like that."

"Wasn't any sneaking involved."

"Anyone else out there with you? Durell maybe? Sandy?"

Hicks shook his head. "Durell's still over there. And I haven't seen Sandy in months."

"Close the door."

Hicks lowered his hands, pulled the door shut behind him.

"Now step over here."

Holding the gun on him, Greggs reached up with his left hand, slapped his sides, his waistband.

"Sad to think we've come to this," Hicks said.

"Whose fault is that?"

"What I'm here to talk about. But not while you're holding that."

Greggs looked at him, then lowered the .45.

"Thanks. Why don't you decock that sumbitch while you're at it?"

Greggs pointed the gun at the floor, used both hands to lower the hammer. They heard the dog bark twice more, then go quiet.

"I'm gonna shoot that thing someday," Greggs said. "I hate that dog."

"You're not shooting anything. Can I sit?"

Greggs nodded at the breakfast nook. Hicks pushed aside dirty laundry, sat facing him. "Maid's on vacation, I see. How long you intend to live out here like this?"

Greggs didn't answer. He put the .45 beside him on the day-bed, next to his cell phone.

"Sharon's worried about you," Hicks said. "That's not very fair to her, is it?"

"She understands. Grab me those butts, will you?"

There was a hard pack of Marlboros beside the prosthetic leg. Hicks picked it up, tossed it into Greggs's lap. He thumbed the box open, took out a cigarette and a cheap plastic lighter.

"So, what?" he said. "I'm supposed to be happy to see you?"

"You should be. I imagine you will be when you hear what I have to say."

"I'm listening." He lit the cigarette, put the lighter back inside, closed the pack.

Hicks picked up the prosthetic leg. It weighed less than he expected. "You don't wear this? It cost Uncle enough."

"It chafes. Itches like a motherfucker, too. Can't seem to get it to fit right." He took an open beer can from the windowsill behind him, wedged it between his thighs.

"Can you walk with it?"

"A little. Not far."

He set the leg back down. "What's the therapist say?"

Greggs blew out smoke, tapped ash in the beer can. "You bring me anything?"

Hicks waved away smoke. "Why I'm here."

"About time."

Hicks reached inside his jacket, and Greggs put his hand on the .45. Hicks drew out the rubber-banded envelope slowly, held it up, then tossed it onto the daybed. "Part of your share. More to come."

"How much is in there?"

"Twenty K, brother. The reason I had to drive my ass all the way up here instead of flying. But like I said, it's only part."

Greggs drew the envelope closer, slipped off the rubber bands. The cigarette bobbed in his lips, ashes falling in his lap. He opened the envelope, looked through the manicured bills.

"Nice and clean," Hicks said.

"I can see that." He riffled the bills with a thumb, closed the envelope again, set it beside the .45. "I've still got thirty coming."

"I know it. He knows it, too."

"You still working for that old bastard?"

"Sometimes. His money's good."

"But he's slow on paying, isn't he? Everything we did for him over there, all that shit we helped bring back. We should've got a bigger cut from all of that. We're the ones took the risks."

"It's never that easy," Hicks said. "Things like that, you have to wait, find the right buyers. Let things cool down before you make a deal, see any money."

"More bullshit."

"But the way you've been going, threatening him, saying shit about talking to the FBI, well, that only makes matters worse."

"I wanted him to know I was serious."

"He knows. That's why he sent me up here with your money. And as soon as he has the other thirty together, I'll bring that up to you, too. Then we're square. But he needs to know you're still on the team, that your allegiances are intact."

"I just want what's owed me, that's all."

"I know. And you'll get it."

Greggs nodded at the kitchenette. "There's beers in there."

"Best thing you've said yet." Hicks got up, bent over and opened the short-boy refrigerator. Inside were four loose Olympia cans, a bottle of peppermint schnapps, and a curling slice of pizza on a paper plate. He took out two cans, kneed the door shut. "I didn't know anybody drank that peppermint shit after high school."

"It does the trick. Keeps me from having to go to bed sober."

Hicks popped a can, foam oozing out. He handed it to Greggs, opened his own, sat back in the breakfast nook.

"Sorry about the smoke," Greggs said. "You're still living healthy, I see, kind of shape you're in."

"I try."

Greggs looked at his cigarette. "I never used to smoke. At least not before I went over there. Now I'm doing like three packs a day. Calms my nerves."

"Must get expensive. The VA rep still come by?" He drank beer. It was thin and lukewarm.

Greggs snorted out smoke. "They're done with me, I think. I did the counseling at first, listened to their bullshit. They wanted me to move back into the house. Sharon did, too. They didn't understand I was just fine out here."

"Maybe you should try to get out more. Be healthier for you. Get some fresh air. Interact with people."

"Fuck people."

"How the neighbors feel about you living in your driveway?"

"Fuck the neighbors, too."

Hicks laughed. "You haven't changed, sure as shit." He sipped beer, nodded at the .45. "Nice weapon—1911? Can I take a look?"

"It's fine where it is. You've seen one before."

"You getting paranoid in middle age, Arlen?"

"Just careful. So where's Durell?"

"Kabul, last I heard."

"You stay in touch?"

"Now and then."

"And Sandoval?"

"Not so much. Sandy's stateside now. We were a good team while it lasted, all of us."

"Until it went to shit," Greggs said, and drank beer.

"We had a good run."

"Yeah, well, I'm not doing much running these days."

"You know what I meant. So what's your plan? Sit around, drink yourself to death?"

"It's a thought."

"You used to be one squared-away motherfucker. What happened?"

"What do you think happened? That good run we had cost some of us more than others, didn't it?"

Hicks ran a thumb around the rim of the can. "You ever tell Sharon anything about all that? Kind of thing we were doing over there?"

Greggs shook his head, tapped ash. "That what you came all the way here to find out? If so, you wasted your time. She doesn't know shit about any of that."

"Just asking," Hicks said. He drank beer, swirled what was left in the can, set it on the table.

"So you came here to pay me, and now you did," Greggs said. "Are we going to sit around now, bullshit about old times?"

"I just wanted to see how you were doing."

"And find out if you could still trust me?"

"That, too."

"You think I can't keep my mouth shut? That if I got pissed off enough about the money, I'd put us all in the shit?"

"I didn't say that."

"You thought it, though."

Hicks stood, put his palms in the small of his back, stretched. "Where's the head in this thing? I've got a long drive back."

Greggs pointed at a narrow door past the kitchenette. Hicks went inside, closed the door, pulled the string to turn on the light. It was no cleaner in there. His shoulders brushed the walls.

He unzipped, urinated loudly into the toilet, knowing Greggs would hear it through the thin door. Then he zipped back up, put his right boot on the toilet seat, pulled up his jeans leg. He drew out the wood-handled ice pick from his boot, took the cork off the tip. Then he flushed, turned the light off, and went back out, the ice pick hidden in his cupped right hand.

Greggs was counting the money, the envelope in his lap. Hicks closed the distance. Greggs looked up at the last moment, reached for the .45. Hicks slapped his left hand over Greggs's mouth, slammed his head back into the wall, and sank the ice pick into the left side of his chest, angling upward to slip between the ribs.

Greggs bucked, his eyes wide. Hicks held him there, leaning all his weight into him, drew out the ice pick and drove it home again.

He felt Greggs's teeth scrape against his palm, trying to bite. He straddled him, used a knee to knock the .45 to the floor. "Easy, Arlen. Easy. Don't fight me."

The ice pick came out and went in again, all the way to the handle this time. Hicks twisted it, felt the wet warmth on his hand.

Greggs groaned into his palm, bucked again, bills falling to the floor, his T-shirt darkening with blood. Hicks got in closer. "It's okay," he said into his ear. "Don't fight it, brother. Don't fight it. Go easy."

Greggs shut his eyes tight, then snapped them open again. Hicks drew out the ice pick, drove it home in a different spot.

Greggs's struggles weakened. His right leg spasmed, the heel tapping the floor. Hicks imagined what was going on inside him, the lungs filling with blood, the heart slowing, sluggish. He drew out the ice pick, took his hand away, stepped back.

Greggs was gasping, dragging in air, blood on his lips. Red bubbles rose through the holes in his T-shirt. Hicks put a hand on his right shoulder, gently pushed him back against the wall again. "Easy, brother."

Hicks traced the red tip of the ice pick across Greggs's chest, to his best guess at where the heart was. He held it there, no pressure yet. Their eyes locked. Greggs's lips were moving.

"Sha . . . ," he breathed. "Shar . . ."

"I'm sorry, man," Hicks said. "I really am." He leaned forward, used his weight to push the ice pick all the way home. Greggs's eyelids fluttered, and then he was still.

Hicks stood back, breathing hard. He drew out the ice pick, looked down at the blood on his hand. He'd been careful, so there was none on his pants, and only a few drops on his jacket sleeve. Nothing anyone would notice at night.

In the kitchenette, he ran water in the small sink, washed the ice pick clean, then his hand. Blood swirled pink in the drain.

He shut off the water, left the ice pick in the sink, dried his hands with a paper towel. Then he went back to the daybed, picked up all the bills, replaced them in the envelope, snapped the rubber bands around it. The envelope went back into his pocket.

He had to move Greggs's body to the side to get the cell phone. It would have his number in it. Even though he'd called from a burner, he didn't want to leave any connection behind. He put the phone with the money.

He used a dirty T-shirt from the breakfast nook to wipe down everything he'd touched. Then he went into the kitchenette, opened the cabinet beneath the stove, and found what he was looking for, the two propane lines coming in from the outside tanks.

Using the T-shirt, he opened drawers, found a pair of pliers in the second one, mixed in with silverware, pens, and small tools. He started to shut the drawer again, saw the edge of the black box stuck in the back. He drew it out, knowing already what it was. He lifted the lid, and inside on a bed of cotton was Greggs's Silver Star, on a red, white, and blue ribbon.

He looked at the medal, then back at Greggs, set the box on the counter.

There was no time to search the camper, see if he'd left notes, a journal. It was time to finish this.

He left two windows partially open for oxygen, closed the rest, then knelt in front of the stove. With the T-shirt covering the pliers' teeth to prevent sparks, he unscrewed the propane lines. Gas began to hiss into the kitchenette, the smell of the odorant making his eyes water.

There was a small toaster oven on the counter. He unplugged it and carried it into the bedroom at the far end of the camper, holding his breath against the gas. Just a mattress on the floor here, tangled sheets, scattered clothes. He set the oven on the floor, then ripped the T-shirt in half and shoved part of it inside, pushing it up against the coils. He plugged the cord into a wall socket, turned the dial to its highest setting, wiped down what he'd touched. The oven began to hum.

He closed the bedroom door to give himself more time, got the ice pick from the sink, and left the camper. Shutting the door tightly behind him, he wiped the outside latch clean, then went down the steps.

There was a single light still on in the house. Sharon waiting up to hear from him. He hadn't wanted it like this, but there was no other way. And he'd have to be quick, before the camper went up.

He held the ice pick down at his side, shoved the torn T-shirt into his jacket pocket. He would need it. As he started up the driveway, the dog began to bark.

SEVEN

Crissa steered the rental car to the side of the road, looked off into the empty desert, heat haze rising, and thought, This is the place.

She got out of the car, taking the binoculars with her. Only forty-five minutes from Las Vegas, the city already out of sight behind the hills. In the distance, snowcapped mountains, but here, only an endless stretch of parched red earth, strewn with boulders.

She'd driven another twenty miles south, still scouting, but hadn't found a better place, so she'd turned around, come back. The land here was mostly flat, but on the other side of the road was an arroyo that ran parallel to the highway. No guardrail, and ten feet deep at least.

On this side was a scattering of rocks, the largest about twelve feet high and twenty feet wide. High-tension lines in the far distance, and about two hundred yards past the rocks a single cell tower, maybe a hundred and fifty feet high, bristling with antennae at different levels. There was a cluster of equipment cabinets in an enclosure at its base, surrounded by a high chain-link fence topped with razor wire.

She wore a black pullover, jeans, and boots, and the heat was a shock after the air-conditioning in the car. From Texas, she'd flown directly to Vegas, picked up the rental. Standing out here now, in the middle of this emptiness, she felt for the first time that it was all real, that it might work.

She heard a distant thrum, looked north and saw a dark shape coming down the road, seeming to rise and fall in the blacktop haze. A tractor-trailer, moving fast. She walked back to the wide boulder. It would be a good vantage point. From here, she could see anything coming down the highway in either direction. The truck blew past, raising dust.

Behind the boulder was a natural depression, already shadowed. She gouged at the ground with a boot heel. Beneath an inch of dusty topsoil, the earth was packed flat and hard. Enough traction for a vehicle, she guessed, especially if it was four-wheel drive.

She pushed her sunglasses up into her hair, raised the binoculars. Empty land in all directions, mountains beyond. To the west, California and the Mojave. To the south, Arizona and, beyond that, Mexico. Above the southern mountains, a white contrail etched slowly across the blue sky, the plane too high to be seen.

She got back in the car, set the binoculars on the seat. It was a new Nissan Altima, fewer than two thousand miles on it, and she'd need to be careful taking it off the road. It would be bad news to get stuck out here in the middle of nowhere, break an axle on a rock, or drive into loose sand she couldn't get out of, have to call for a tow.

She started the engine, pulled slowly off the shoulder and into the dirt, the car rising and falling on the uneven ground. Once behind the boulder, she backed and filled until the entire car was in shadow. With the motor running, she got out, walked north up the highway for about two hundred feet, looked back. Standing on the center line, she couldn't see the Nissan at all. She went another hundred feet, where the angle of the road changed, but the car was still hidden.

She walked in the other direction, stopped, looked back, went fifty feet more and did it again. The car was out of sight from all angles. It would do.

She got back in the car, put it in gear. The rear tires bit the ground easily, with no fishtailing. She pulled out of the shelter of the rock, back onto the solid ground of the shoulder, and parked.

The digital camera she'd brought was cheap, but good enough for her purposes. She took it from the glove box, got out of the car, and began snapping pictures in all directions. Wide landscape shots at first, then details: the surface of the road, the loose stones on the shoulder, the hollow behind the boulder. She walked out toward the cell tower, took distance shots before moving in closer. Inside the chain-link fence, squat boxes of machinery hummed. On one of them a bright yellow sign with a black lightning bolt warned DANGER! HIGH VOLTAGE!

Something moved in her peripheral vision, and she turned to see a jackrabbit run past, then vanish into an unseen hole. The wind whined through the razor wire. A tumbleweed blew against the chain-link.

She walked back to the road, her shadow stretching out in front of her. In the coolness of the car, she got out her cell phone and dialed Hicks's number.

When he answered, she said, "I found it. You need to come take a look."

"When? Where?"

"As soon as you can. And I'll show you when you get here."

"I've been traveling," he said. "I just got back to—"

"Call me when you get to Vegas," she said, and hung up.

At the motel restaurant, she sat at a table near the big window, looked out at dark mountains, lightning pulsing in the clouds. The motel was thirty miles from the spot she'd picked, set back from the highway and close to the hills. She'd finished her dinner, was on her second glass of wine. Her work for the day was done. She could relax until she heard from Hicks.

The restaurant was dark paneling, wagon-wheel chandeliers. There was a bar beyond, through a short hallway and swinging saloon doors. Noise coming out of there, laughter, and country music from a jukebox.

Occasionally a tractor-trailer rolled by on the interstate, rattling the chandeliers. Other than that, it was blackness out there, broken only by flashes of dry lightning that, for all she knew, were a hundred miles away.

"Ma'am, I couldn't help but notice you're all by yourself out here."

She looked up. The man was in his fifties maybe, thin, wearing cowboy boots, a Western shirt with snap buttons, a belt buckle in the shape of a pair of dice. His hair was combed back and cut with silver, and he held a black felt cowboy hat at his side. Being a gentleman.

"What I'd like to do," he said, "is buy you another glass of whatever it is you're drinking there."

"Thank you. But I'm just about to call it a night. Maybe some other time."

"Not even one glass? It's still early, and I'd hate to have to drink alone."

"Thanks, but no."

"Well, allow me to introduce myself at least," he said. "My name is—" He started to draw out a chair. She hooked a foot around one of its legs, stopped him.

"Drift," she said.

He met her eyes, saw something there he wasn't used to. He straightened, looked down at her, his smile gone. He gave a slight bow, turned away, said, "Dyke," under his breath, and went back down the hallway and through the saloon doors. She watched him go, wondering if he was staying at the motel, if he might be a problem later.

Her cell buzzed. She pulled it from her jeans pocket. Hicks's number.

"Where are you?" she said.

"Still in L.A. Can't get a flight until tomorrow." His voice flat, tired.

"Everything okay?"

"Everything's fine. I just had something to do last night, and a long drive afterward. It's all straightened out now."

"I'll pick you up at the airport," she said. "Better to have just one car when we go out to the site; it'll attract less attention. Call me when you have your flight info. I'll get you another room where I'm staying. It'll be easier."

"We coming back here afterward? To L.A.?"

"You are," she said. "Not me."

"Why not?"

"There's somebody I have to go see first."

Hicks walked down the center of the road, put his hands on his hips, turned slowly, squinted back to where she stood by the boulder, the Nissan parked out of sight behind it.

"You're right," he said. "It could work."

He started back toward her. He looked tired. Hungover, she guessed, the faint scent of alcohol and sweat coming from his skin.

"Still," he said. "A straightway like this, vehicles build up some speed. A curve in the road would make it easier to stop them. Especially three vehicles at once."

"There's ways to do that. We don't need a curve."

He looked north. "Closer to Vegas than I'd like."

"It's the best place for what we're talking about."

"Lots of open country. That convoy could go off-road, haul ass across the flat. Be hard to chase it."

"They won't have the chance," she said. "We're going to box them in."

"How?"

She pointed at the mountains to the north.

"That's the way they'll be coming. There's a turnoff way back there, at the base of those hills, that goes up into some rocks. I already checked it out. We can hide a vehicle there. When the tail car goes by, our car swings out after it, keeping enough distance so no one gets nervous. They follow it all the way here. When we stop the convoy, our car comes up close behind the tail car, blocks it in. We do it right, all three vehicles will be bunched together. They won't be going anywhere."

"And how do we stop them? Spike strips? Pull another vehicle out in the middle of the road, block it off?"

"Neither," she said. "We can't take a chance with either of those. If there's a collision, and one of our own cars gets disabled out here, we're out of luck. What we need to do . . ." She walked south down the road, past the boulder. He followed. ". . . is stop the lead car right about here."

"Again, how?"

"With something in the road that distracts them. Causes a big enough scare that they hit the brakes, but with enough lead time so the other vehicles don't pile into them. We get the people out and contained, then my guy drives the truck away. We disable the other two cars, get them off the road. Then we take off in different directions."

He nodded, looked around, turned back to her. "Any ideas on what that distraction might be?"

"That would be your department."

He looked at her for a moment, then smiled. "IED. That's what you're thinking."

"Maybe."

"And you're assuming I know how to make one."

"Don't you?"

"Maybe. But that kind of thing can be unpredictable. There's always the risk of collateral damage."

"That's why it needs to be small scale," she said. "Something that gets their attention, but gives them time to stop. We don't want to flip a vehicle or send it skidding off the road. Last thing we need is to have to pull that truck out of a ravine. It has to be something that can be set off safely, by someone who's got a good eye, who can measure the distance and pick the right moment. Not too soon, not too late. And whatever it is, it can't cause any significant damage to the road. We'll need it ourselves."

"You're good at this," he said. "The planning."

"That's why he hired me."

They saw a tractor-trailer coming from the south, stepped back off the highway. Hicks stuck his hands in the back pockets of his jeans, toed loose stones with his boot, watched the truck go by, trailing dust behind it.

When it was gone, he cocked his head at the cell tower. "What about that?"

"One of the reasons I picked this spot. It's the only tower around for almost ten miles."

"How's that help us?"

"If it were out of commission," she said, "chances are, you wouldn't be able to get a signal here. A half mile down the road, in either direction, it might be a different story. But right here, in this spot"—she nodded at the road—"it's the only game in town."

He looked at the tower, the equipment surrounding it.

"Maybe we can find a way to jam signals in and out of it," she said. "Just long enough to do what we need to."

"Too subtle for me. I wouldn't know the first thing about that. But I've dealt with this situation before."

"And?"

"See all those units at the base?" he said. "That's the equipment compound. Out here in the middle of nowhere, that tower has to be self-sufficient. It'll use a lot of power, not just to relay signals, but to keep the whole thing cool. And since Katrina, a lot of cell towers have eight-hour power backups—batteries, additional generators, whatever."

"Security cameras?"

"Not that I know of. And I don't see any there."

"So how do we cut the power?"

"Couple of grenades over that fence might do it. Maybe some C-4, take the whole thing down, let someone else clean up the mess."

"No good. Too much noise, too much smoke. They'll see it for miles."

"A lighter touch, then. We cut through the fence, lay a couple small charges, blow out the utility supply and the gens. Either way, they'll know when that thing goes off-line. It'll set off alarms back at their network operations center, wherever that is. They'll send someone out to check."

"We'll be out of here by then," she said. "You see enough?"

"I think so, for now." They started back to the car.

"We'll head back toward Vegas," she said. "I'll show you where that turnoff is, where we'll pick up the convoy. I've got photos of everything. When we get back to the motel, we can go over the final route on a map."

"I could do with a drink, too."

"You look like you had enough last night."

"I had my reasons."

They got in the car, and she started the engine. He looked off across the desert to the cell tower, outlined against the hard blue sky. "It's really happening, isn't it?"

"Not unless we make it happen," she said. "And we do that one step at a time."

EIGHT

When they got back to the motel, she showered and changed, then called Walt Rathka, the lawyer she used in New York. Monique, his secretary, put her through.

"I was going to call you," he said. "But I wasn't sure if I had a working number."

"This one's good for a couple days. I'll call when I have a new one."

"This one safe?"

"Safe enough."

She pictured him in his office, twelve stories above Fifth Avenue, sitting behind the big oak desk. For the last ten years, he'd handled her take-home cash, investing it in legitimate businesses, mostly strip malls and car washes in the South. He also moved her money through various accounts, including one she kept at a bank in St. Lucia.

"Those wire transfers you were waiting on came through," he said.

Cota's down payment. "Good. How much?"

"Just as you said. Four deposits, twenty-five K each. They've cleared already."

"Where'd they go?"

"Offshore at the moment. You want me to take some, put it to work?"

"No," she said. "Let it sit for now. I'll figure out what I want to do later."

"You home?"

"No."

"Working?"

"Maybe."

"You know, the books look good. You might not need to for a while. I can always shift some funds around if you need access. No reason to go out again so soon. And, to be honest, I'd be happier if you didn't."

"This was unexpected," she said. "But it might work out."

"Let me know when you're back home. And safe."

"I will," she said.

They were in Crissa's room, the map spread out on the table. She'd marked the route with a yellow highlighter, penciled in distances.

They'd had dinner and one drink each in the restaurant, then bought bottles at the packaged goods store across the highway. Wine for her, a small bottle of Johnnie Walker Red for him. They drank from plastic motel glasses. He'd gotten ice from the machine by the office, half filled his cup with it before adding whisky. She stood. He straddled a chair.

"How many miles altogether?" he said. "From the warehouse to the spot you picked?"

"About forty. But what's more important is the distance from the turnoff where we stash the truck, to the spot where we'll be waiting. That's fifteen miles, so figure twenty minutes to close that distance. We'll know the convoy's coming, and we'll be able to see them long before they reach us, so we'll be ready. We'll have to be, because we'll only get one chance to stop them."

He nodded, looked at the map, swirled the ice in his glass.

"Questions?" she said, and drank wine. It was her second glass since they'd come back to the room, and she was feeling it now, a faint sense of light-headedness and warmth.

He shook his head. "Not right now. I will, though."

"You pick your other man yet?"

"I called him. He's on board. And solid. He'll be fine."

"He serve with you?"

"Yeah. In the Corps, and then again when we were PMCs. I brought him into that. He's a professional."

"He'll keep his cool when things jump off?"

"Count on it. You're under fire with a man more than once, you learn a lot about his character. You want to vet him?"

She shook her head, began to fold up the map. "Not necessary. I trust you."

"And Emile will make it worth his while. He won't have any gripes, before or after. Maximum pay, minimal work."

"Will he make it worth your while, too?"

"He always does."

She sat on the edge of the bed. "It's your business, but I'm curious. You get a piece of what he's earning from this?"

"Doesn't work like that."

"Flat fee? That doesn't bother you?" Sounding him out, now that his guard was down.

"His business is his business. I'm strictly a working man, and that's the way I like it."

"You're a mercenary."

He drank his scotch. "I guess you could put it that way."

"There another way to put it?"

"You have a problem with that? Aren't you the same thing?"

"Relax. No offense intended."

He put his glass on the table, arched his back, raised his arms and stretched without standing. She watched his muscles flex.

"Anything else you want to ask me?" he said. "If so, now's the time." He picked up the glass again.

"What do you hope to get from working for him? I mean, in the long run?"

"A nest egg. With what he's been paying me, I'm almost where I need to be."

"To do what?"

"Start my own agency, hire some young bucks who know an MRE from an RPG. Maybe some women, too. They're generally smarter anyway, I've found. Then I'll just sit home all day, watch the money roll in."

"Would it be that easy?"

"It could be. If you're lucky, and you know what you're doing. And I'm both."

She smiled at that.

"You disagree?" he said. "What do you think I am?"

She set her glass on the nightstand. "You want me to be honest?"

"Of course."

"I think you're lonely and horny and dangerous."

She looked at him, waited for his response. He didn't smile. He held her eyes for a moment. "Well, two out of three maybe," he said, and drank.

"Sorry. Tell me more about Cota."

"You know a lot already. What more do you want?"

"What's the deal with that maid? Katya, that her name?"

"She's been with him a long time. Since she was about eighteen, I think."

"They sleep together?"

"At some point, probably. But now, who knows? His business, not mine. He treats me well, that's all I care about. But yeah, he had his wild years, I'm sure. And good for him."

"What about you? Ever married, kids?"

He shook his head.

"Never?"

"Never had time."

"Brothers, sisters?"

"Brother somewhere up in Oregon, haven't seen him in years. No sisters."

"Parents?"

"Both gone."

"What did your father do?"

He looked at her, an expression she couldn't read.

"You said I could ask you anything," she said.

He set the glass back down. "What did my old man do? He drank mostly, got in bar fights. He was in the Corps, too. Vietnam.

He was in Da Nang, a bunch of other places. Then, when I was sixteen, he took the government-issue .45 he'd smuggled back . . ."

He made a gun with his right hand, touched the index finger to his temple, and dropped the thumb.

"I'm sorry," she said.

"No reason to be. Now, if you're asking if Emile's some kind of father figure, you can leave off that right now. I had a father. I'm not looking for another one."

"I wasn't going to say that."

"He pays me well, and I do what he needs me to do. And occasionally . . ." He stood. ". . . I have to do some shit I don't necessarily want to do. But that's just the way it goes."

He went over to the dresser where the bottles were, looked at her. She nodded, handed him her glass. He poured wine, then dropped ice in his own glass, filled it with scotch. He took the drinks back, handed hers over, sat. The room felt warmer, the wine getting to her. She'd have to be careful.

"I'm still not used to that black hair," he said. "I bet there's a story goes with that, too."

"There is. But the color'll wash out soon. It'll be back to what it was."

"I'd ask you more about yourself, but I have the feeling I wouldn't get very far."

"There's not much to tell."

"That's hard to believe."

"I was wondering," she said, steering him away. "You said you work for Cota, do what he asks, get paid. Would you work for anybody?"

"That depends."

"Anybody that paid well enough?"

"Probably."

"Would you work for Iran? North Korea?"

He grinned. "What makes you think I haven't already?"

"Which one?"

"I'm just kidding. I have my standards. They couldn't afford me anyway."

He finished his drink, leaned forward to toss the glass into the wastebasket by the nightstand.

"You're an interesting man," she said.

"Not really."

She looked at her watch, felt a faint pulse of guilt seeing the tattoo on her wrist. "It's getting late."

"So it is. Too bad we're on separate flights tomorrow."

"Better that way."

He got to his feet, unsteady for a moment, gripped the back of the chair for support. "Leg's asleep."

"Be careful."

He nodded, gave her a crooked smile. "See you in the morning."

"Right."

She watched him leave, the door shutting behind him.

She put her glass on the nightstand, got up, feeling a rush of blood to her head. The wine bottle on the dresser was almost empty. She couldn't remember the last time she'd been drunk.

She chained the door, hooked the night latch, then undressed. She stood under the shower for a long time, turned to let the needling spray play along her back. Dark water ran around her feet, more dye washing out.

The knocking was faint at first, the shower noise almost drowning it out. She twisted off the faucet, listened. It came again, a light tapping.

She stepped out of the shower, toweled quickly, then slipped on her bathrobe, tied the belt. She went out into the room, feet wet on the carpet.

At the door, she looked through the spyhole. Hicks stood in the light there, one hand propped on the door frame, his body wide and distorted by the glass.

She closed her eyes, took a breath, then undid the chain and the latch, opened the door.

"I forgot my bottle," he said, and gestured toward the nightstand.

She held the door wider. When she didn't move, he bit his lip, looked at her, said, "Sorry. I made a mistake."

"No," she said. "You didn't."

He came in, and she closed the door behind him.

She lay awake, listened to the far-off sound of trucks on the highway. Hicks snored softly beside her, one arm around a pillow, the other thrown across her waist. The room was dark except for the light from the bathroom. She touched the back of his right shoulder, traced the tattoo there, a grinning skull with tiger fangs.

He didn't stir when she lifted his arm gently and slid out from beneath it. She went naked into the bathroom, shut the door. In the mirror, the fluorescent light gave her skin a yellowish cast.

This was a mistake, she thought. You need to keep your head clear, and your eyes open. This can't happen again.

She drank tap water from her cupped palms, splashed some on her face, hearing Wayne's voice in her head.

Someday you're going to have to make a choice.

NINE

She pulled the rental Dodge up to the wooden gates, flashed her headlights twice. Beyond, a long gravel driveway led down to the farmhouse. There was a single light on in a second-floor window. It had taken her a half hour to drive here from Cincinnati.

On the seat beside her, her cell buzzed. When she answered, Bobby Chance said, "That you out there, Red?"

"IRS. We want that two million buried in your backyard."

He laughed. "I wish. Gate's unlocked. Come on up."

She got out, pushed open the double gates. They were hinged onto head-high pillars, part of the rough stone wall that ran around the property.

She drove past the gates, got out again and pushed them shut. There was a barrel-bolt lock on this side, a hasp where a padlock would go.

A light went on in the side yard of the house, illuminating a blue pickup truck. She got back in the Dodge, drove slowly, gravel crackling under the tires. Any vehicle going in or out of here would make a lot of noise. On either side of the driveway, the land sloped down to a pair of retention ponds, black water and weeds.

The house was old, shaded by live oaks that nearly hid it from view. As she neared it, she saw that the driveway curved past it and ended in a clearing in front of a faded-red barn. Beyond that, a cultivated field stretched out to a dark treeline. No other lights out there. No neighbors.

She drove toward the pickup, saw a shadow move out from behind one of the trees. A man with a gun.

She braked easily, then powered down her window. Chance stepped into the light, grinning, a pistol at his side, and said, "Long time."

"Too long," she said.

"Not so red these days."

"Dye," she said. "It's almost gone."

They were at the kitchen table. He'd put the gun, a snub-nosed .38, atop the refrigerator. The woman he'd introduced as Lynette set steaming mugs of coffee in front of them, turned her back to pour another from the automatic brewer. She was in her early twenties, with long brown hair, wearing a sweatshirt and blue jeans.

Chance's hair was buzz-cut, the shortest she'd ever seen it. He wore a red flannel shirt, the sleeves rolled back to show the tattoos on his arms, elaborate designs he'd spent thousands on in Thailand.

"You look good," Crissa said.

"You too."

"How's the arm?"

He rubbed his right shoulder, rolled the joint there. "A little stiff sometimes, especially when it's cold out. Rotator cuff got chewed up, so I can't raise it as high as I used to. Couple pellets still floating around in there, too."

The last time they'd worked together had been a takeover at a card game in Florida that had gone bad. A man had followed them back north to recover the money. It had all ended on a cold day in Connecticut, and Chance had taken a shotgun blast to the shoulder before she'd killed the man who'd hunted them. She'd dropped Chance outside a hospital emergency room that night, hadn't seen him since.

Lynette turned to them, mug in hand. "I'm not sure I want to hear all this. I'll be out in the living room. Call me if you need me." She left the room.

Crissa watched her go. "I hope it's not a problem, my being here."

"No," he said. "It's just . . . Never mind." He got up, took a sugar bowl from the counter, two spoons from a drawer. "Milk?"

"No. I'm good."

He sat back down. "I told her I'm out of the Game. Told Sladden the same thing."

"He didn't want to pass my number on to you at first," she said. "Didn't say why."

"That's why."

She nodded at the hallway. "She know about before? What you used to do?"

"Some of it." He stirred sugar into his coffee. "She's a smart girl. She would have figured it out anyway, how I could afford this place. Not that it's in my name."

"How's that work?"

"Shell company, an LLC out of Cleveland. On the books, they own the house, all the land."

"You're growing something out there."

"Soy," he said. "I lease out that field. I have a tenant farmer does the planting and harvesting, takes care of the land. I wouldn't know what to do with it myself. All I do is cash his check every month."

She touched her own shoulder. "Lynette know how that happened?"

"Yeah."

"Another reason she doesn't like me."

"You're the first person from that part of my life she's met. I told her I was done, and I meant it. I can't blame her for being angry."

"The fact I'm a woman probably doesn't help either."

He blew on his coffee. "What's in the bag?"

She lifted the olive-drab backpack she'd carried in from the car, set it on the table. "Money."

"For who?"

"You. Ten thousand. That's what I got for the Mustang."

He grinned. "I'd almost forgotten all about that."

After Connecticut, she'd taken his car, fled south. She'd sold the Mustang to a dealer in Columbia, South Carolina, no questions asked.

"Your car," she said. "Your money."

"That's a hoot. You come all the way to Ohio to give me that?"

"That, and to run a couple things by you." She sipped coffee. It was bitter and dark.

He turned to look back down the hallway, then inched his chair closer to the table. "I wasn't shining her on. I am out."

"I understand. But I feel like I owe you something, too."

"What?"

"An easy payday, maybe."

"Is there such a thing?"

"Some are easier than others."

He sat back. She spooned sugar into her mug, stirred, steam rising up.

"I had a visit a while back," he said. "From a mutual friend of ours, Larry Black. I met him in town. Lynette didn't know about it."

She lifted her mug but didn't drink.

"He was out here looking at some work," he said. "Fell through, I guess. At least I never heard from him again."

"He's dead."

"You know that for a fact?"

"I was there."

"You were working?"

"Detroit. It went well, and then it didn't."

"What happened?"

"Two amateurs got involved. They're both dead now, too, as far as I know."

"Well, that's something."

"If I'd played it better, it might have gone differently. Larry would still be alive."

"You don't know that. And anyway, he knew the risks. We all do."

She drank coffee. "You've got a nice setup here."

"It's quiet," he said. "I'm finding I like that more and more as I get older."

"One way in and out, though. That would make me nervous."

"There's another road 'round back," he said. "Through the trees. That's how my tenant brings his equipment in. I could keep those front gates locked all the time, still get in or out as I need to."

"Smart."

"So tell me about this payday."

She looked down the darkness of the hall, could see the flickering light of a television. "Sure you want to hear it?"

"You came all this way. And you're staying here tonight, right?"

She shook her head. "I have a motel in town. Better that way. I don't want to cause any trouble."

"It wouldn't be any trouble, but it's up to you. Now go on."

"I need a driver," she said. "Someone good under pressure, who can think on his feet. You're the first one came to mind."

"What kind of vehicle?"

"A truck."

"Tractor-trailer?"

"Smaller."

"A hijack?"

"More like a give-up."

"What's the exposure?"

"Taking it? Five minutes at most. Then a short drive and a transfer to a clean truck. After the transfer, you drive the second truck a hundred miles or so to a designated spot, leave it, then you're home free. We'll work out picking you up, getting you on a plane. You could be back here that same night."

"That's the risk, what's the reward?"

"A hundred K. Ten minutes' work, then two hours, maybe, driving."

"You're running this, I take it."

"I am. But there's a money man behind it. Fifty K when you sign on, fifty when it's done. And I make sure everybody gets paid."

"How many in the crew?"

"You, me, two others I'll pick. If you have suggestions after I've laid it all out for you, let me know. The banker will also have a couple people along."

"Not sure I like that idea."

"They're ex-military," she said. "Pros."

"What branch?"

"Marines, like you."

He sat back, crossed his arms. "More brothers gone bad."

"They've been out for a while, working private. They know their stuff. And as far as the work goes, they'll answer to me. They're there for support, that's all."

"How much are they getting?"

"Not my bother. Employer's taking care of that."

He rocked back on the chair legs, looked at the ceiling.

"No pressure," she said. "You say no, and that's it. We have a nice visit, maybe the three of us have some dinner tomorrow. Then I'm on a flight back to New Jersey. No issues."

"Jersey, that where you're living now?"

"More or less. Think about it tonight, if you want to. And if you're out, you're out. I understand."

He set the chair back down, stirred his coffee. "What do you hear from Wayne?"

She looked down at her mug. "Saw him a few days ago."

"How's he making out?"

"Hanging in. Like he always says, one day at a time."

"Larry Black told me what happened, about his sentence being extended. It was a fight?"

"He had a beef with some Aryans. Decided to take it to them. It was stupid. His parole was coming up."

"He called his own play, I guess. How's it look now?"

"Not good. He's lucky the other man lived. But he'll max out his sentence now, maybe another five on top of that, before he gets out. There was nothing I could do."

"How was he when you saw him? How'd he seem?"

"Like he'd given up." She drank coffee.

"I'm sorry to hear that."

"He made his choice."

He shook his head slowly. "Hell of a thing. So, this other gig, you've got it all worked out already?"

"I will. There's still some issues to deal with."

He exhaled. "One thing I have to say, you were always good with the details. Like Wayne used to say, 'Fail to prepare . . .'"

"'. . . and prepare to fail.' I haven't forgotten that. I haven't forgotten anything he taught me."

"Well," he said, "if we do have dinner"—he nodded at the backpack—"it's on me."

Back at the motel, she put on sweats and T-shirt, stretched on the carpet. Right leg extended, she held the ankle with both hands, touched her head to her knee, feeling the tension in her lower back, the arthritic ache in her hip. Her own souvenir from Connecticut, when she'd been clipped by a car driven by the man who'd come to kill them.

She stretched some more, then got slowly to her feet, legs sore. She was too tired to shower. With the lights off, she lay on the bed, used the remote to flip aimlessly through the channels for a few minutes, then turned off the set again.

Her cell lay dark and silent on the nightstand. Without thinking, she picked it up, opened it, hit POWER. She was low on minutes, would need another burner soon.

She found Hicks's number, wondered where he was right then, what he was doing, who he was with. She remembered the feel of his hands on her, the heat of his touch.

Her thumb hovered over the CALL button for a long moment. Then she closed the phone, pressed POWER again, watched the display fade to black.

TEN

Sandoval opened the back door of the Jaguar, threw in his duffel bag, then got in front with Hicks, said, "About fucking time."

Hicks pulled away from the curb, eased the car into the line of traffic leaving the airport.

"I thought about waiting inside with the limo drivers," Hicks said. "Holding up a sign that said ASSHOLE."

"You probably carry one all the time, right? In case you forget your name?"

Hicks laughed. "It's good to see you, partner, seriously. How's it swinging?"

"Same old, *jefe*. Working for the Man and getting paid. But right now, I need a drink, a meal, and a woman."

"In that order?"

"Whatever. I'm flexible."

"I'll cover the drink and the meal. You're on your own with the woman."

They were almost at the airport exit, the traffic moving faster now. Hicks shifted and pulled ahead, changing lanes. Sandoval looked out the window.

"Been a long time since I been out here, man. It looks the same."

"It always is. Where are you now?"

"Dallas, most of the time. But I spent part of the year working for a mining firm up in Wisconsin, walking around in a balaclava and a boonie hat, carrying an M-16, scaring off the tree huggers. Colder than my ex-wife's *concha* up there."

"That pay?"

"Not as righteous as a PSD, but it kept me going. What's this deal you've got?"

"Crowd control," Hicks said. "Fifteen minutes' work, tops."

"It legal?"

Hicks looked straight ahead, didn't answer.

"Ha," Sandoval said. "I should have known. That three grand you sent got me on the plane, though. So keep talking, *jefe*. Tell me what you need."

They were at a taco stand in East L.A., food in red plastic baskets lined with waxed paper, beer in plastic mugs. They'd taken the farthest table from the takeout window, on the edge of the parking lot. On the stucco wall behind them was a mural of the Virgin Mary, looking up, arms outstretched. Her bare feet pinned a fanged snake to the earth.

"You hear from any of the others?" Sandoval said. "Doctor Shock? Cochise?" He'd left his jacket in the car, wore a black linen shirt open at the throat, showing a white V-neck T-shirt and gold cross beneath.

Hicks shook his head. "Not for a long time."

"Durell and I kept in touch for awhile, e-mail mostly," Sandoval said. "I tried to get him up with me for that mine gig, but he had something else going on. Nobody's hurting for work. I tell you, man, I was scared to death first time I got deployed. Just a kid, you know? Turns out it was the best thing ever happened to me."

Hicks sipped beer, looked across the parking lot.

"You keep watching that car," Sandoval said. "I don't blame you. I'm surprised no one's tried to boost it while we're sitting here. *Cholos* down here probably have that thing chopped for parts in ten minutes. You carrying?"

"In the car."

"You got a CCP?"

"Yeah. Easier than you'd think out here, as long as you have good cause. My last few job descriptions, that hasn't been a problem."

"You hear anything from Greggs?"

Hicks shrugged, pushed his basket away.

"I heard he went off the reservation," Sandoval said.

"Big time. But I saw him awhile back, got it straightened out. Last I heard, he was out in the Midwest somewhere, contemplating his sins."

"He still married?"

"Far as I know."

"He called me up one night when I was in Dallas, drunk, bitching about money that was owed him. I told him if he was smart, he'd keep his mouth shut."

"He had his issues," Hicks said. "But it's all in the past now."

"Hate to see a brother lose it like that, though. You still working for the old man?"

"Yeah. Now and then he finds shit for me to do. It's mostly low stress."

"So tell it. What's the job?"

Hicks's cell began to buzz in his jeans pocket. He took it out, looked at the number. Crissa. He hit QUIET, then turned off the phone, set it on the table.

"For a man with your skill set," he said, "it'll be like once around the park getting a hand job. Trust me."

"Just the two of us?"

"There's some others involved. Independents."

"Contractors?"

"Civilians."

"Fuck that, man. You want real *hombres,* some trigger pullers know their shit, say the word. I make a phone call, get all the guys you want."

"We'll keep it the way it is for now," Hicks said. "See how it goes. I got you a hotel downtown. You get settled today, we'll go over the whole thing tomorrow."

"How soon is this thing happening?"

"About three weeks, but there's a lot to do."

"What about equipment? Ordnance?"

"I've got that taken care of."

"No shit? Good stuff?"

"The best. HK-416s. M-4A's, anything we need."

"Sounds like you're living large out here, Sarge."

"You got enough money to spend," Hicks said, "you can always find a seller, whatever it is you want."

"Why I love this country. So what exactly are we doing?"

"Look at it this way," Hicks said. "Nothing we haven't done before."

* * *

Crissa watched Chance's pickup pull into the motel parking lot, put down her phone. Hicks's line had rung twice. When it went to voice mail, she'd hung up.

She was sitting at a concrete table near the closed pool. A sunny day, but a chill in the air, no one else around. The closeness of the room had started to get to her. Restless, she'd taken the phone outside to make her calls.

Chance parked, came over, sat across from her without a word.

"You look tired," she said.

"I am."

"I caused you trouble last night."

"It wasn't your fault."

"How'd it go with Lynette?"

"About as expected. Pretended to be asleep when I got into bed. Lit into me today. Hard to blame her."

"So I guess dinner's off."

He smiled, pulled a bent pack of Kents from his shirt pocket, lit one with a plastic lighter.

"Since when?" she said.

"These? Since last night. I mean, I quit for a while. Got started a while back, when I got out of the hospital. Nerves. Thought I'd kicked it, though."

"You never told me what happened," she said. "After that night."

He blew out smoke.

"They kept me in the hospital a couple weeks. Police questioned me. A Connecticut statie named Gaitano did most of the talking. I told them I was walking through the woods, got shot. Never saw who did it. Hunters all over the place up there, so it wasn't too much of a stretch. Eventually they bought it. Nothing tied me to what happened at the house, what they found there."

"That's good."

"They didn't want to let me go at first. But I got my lawyer on the phone. He came up and got me. After they cut me loose, I went back to Ohio, did some private rehab there, PT. That's when this started." He raised the cigarette.

"I feel like I'm screwing things up for you again," she said. "I'm sorry."

"Nothing to be sorry about. I owe you."

"No. It's the other way around."

He looked away. "When are you leaving?"

"Tonight."

"Then I guess we're down to it."

"We are."

"And you're waiting on me."

She didn't answer.

He dropped the cigarette on the concrete, ground it out with a heel. "Where's your base for this thing?"

"Outside Vegas. That's where I'm headed."

"Even if I come along," he said, "you still need a couple more people, right? You have anyone in mind?"

"Not yet. I was going to reach out to Sladden, see who's up."

"Any special skills you're looking for?"

"Just a cool head, and the ability to follow directions."

"Ever work with a guy named Keegan, out of Boston?"

"No."

"Irish, a few years older than us."

"I thought you were out of the Game."

"I am. But he and I did something together a few years back, up in Rhode Island. Before that mess in Lauderdale."

"He good?"

"Yeah, he was. Things got crazy, but he kept his end together. We all got paid. Quiet, doesn't talk much, but a good guy to have around if things start going sideways."

"You know how to reach him?"

"Sladden would. I don't know that Keegan's still around, but if he is, Sladden can find him."

"I'll check with him."

"Then I guess I better make up my mind, right?" He got out the cigarettes again.

"You can say no."

"I could."

"If things are going well here, why take the chance?"

"The truth? Kitty's getting low. I pay the mortgage on that farm, taxes, insurance, whatever, even though my name's not on it. Take care of Lynette, too, whatever she needs. Sooner or later, it's gonna be a forced call, I'll need to do something." He lit the cigarette. "What kind of time frame are you looking at?"

"Three weeks, give or take. But if you do drive that truck, once you get it where it's going, you're done. There won't be anybody looking for you. Nothing that connects you to what happened."

"How's the money work?"

"The banker moves the cash into an offshore account I keep. I'll pay you out of that, however you want it. Fifty K when you're on board, another fifty when we're done. I'm the buffer between the money man and the crew. He pays me, I pay you."

"Can you trust him?"

"So far. He's already put up my half. But it'll be my responsibility to make sure everyone gets paid. One way or another, it'll happen."

"How soon could I get that fifty?"

"A few days, I'd think."

He rubbed his tattooed forearm. "It would soften the blow for Lynette, have a check for fifty grand show up."

"More like six separate checks, all under ten thousand. Better that way. Spread it out, maybe different accounts. Keep a low profile."

"Right."

"I'll have a new cell tomorrow. I'll call you. You can give me your answer when you're ready."

He looked at the ground, shook his head.

"What?" she said. She'd never seen him like this before. Wondered what it was he'd lost that night in Connecticut, those long weeks in rehab.

"I think I'd rather leave tonight, "he said. "With you. I'll call Lynette tomorrow from wherever I am."

"Isn't that a little harsh?"

"It'll eliminate some drama, maybe. And to be honest, if I wait until tomorrow, I might change my mind."

"I understand."

He stood. "I'm going to head back now, get my things together."

"You sure?"

"I'm sure. What about iron? I have that .38. A shottie upstairs, too."

"No need," she said. "Someone else is taking care of all that."

He dropped the cigarette, ground it out. "I'll hit you on your cell tonight. Let you know when I'll be ready."

"You don't need to do this."

"I don't know," he said. "I'm thinking maybe I do."

She was having dinner in a coffee shop on the highway when her phone buzzed. Hicks's number. She looked at it, let it ring six times before she answered.

"I called you earlier," she said.

"I know. I'm sorry, got tied up. How are things going?"

"Making progress. You?"

"Same. I'm looking over the equipment list you gave me. There's some things we'll need to talk about. You getting your people together?"

"Working on it."

"My other man's here. He's good to go."

"Once my people commit, we'll need to see those advances," she said. "Sooner rather than later."

"I'll tell him."

Silence on the line.

What?" she said.

"It's just . . . Hell, I was thinking about the other night."

"What about it?"

"Things are a little awkward, I know. And you have that situation down in Texas . . ."

"What's that got to do with anything?"

"It's just . . . It felt pretty special, you know. But at the same time, I don't want it to cause any problems."

"That's not your responsibility. But don't worry about it. It won't."

"I know, but—"

"Listen, Randall. What happened happened. We're adults. Maybe it was a mistake, maybe it wasn't. Doesn't matter. All that matters now is the work."

"I know."

"So let's focus on that, and leave the rest for later."

"I just didn't want there to be any misunderstandings."

"There aren't. I'll call you when I'm in place."

"All right," he said, and she ended the call.

Hicks closed his phone, left the balcony and went back through the French doors. Cota was in a chair by the fireplace, cane across his lap, glass in his hand. The drinks tray was on the table. He looked up when Hicks came in, raised an eyebrow.

"She says it's moving along. But her people will need their money soon."

"They'll get it. What's that look on your face?"

"Nothing." He took another chair. "Just trying to figure some things out." He dropped ice cubes into a glass, poured scotch.

"You're drinking more than usual. Should I be alarmed?"

"I could ask you the same."

"I'll admit to some nervousness. But I have a good feeling about this. It may be early days, but the foundation is solid. And you can build nothing in the absence of a strong foundation."

Hicks held the bottle toward him. Cota nodded. Hicks poured into his glass, set the bottle back down.

"And how is our Miss Wynn doing?" Cota said. "Unless, of

course, your persuasive powers have gotten her to offer up her real name."

"Okay, I gather, from what she said. She'll call me when she's settled."

"I don't think I've ever met anyone quite like her. An unusual woman."

"She is that."

"You seem distracted."

"Just tired." He drank.

"Are you sleeping with her?"

Hicks looked at him.

"I wouldn't think that a difficult question to answer," Cota said.

"Why would you ask?"

"It could become a complication down the road, don't you think? Perhaps it's something best avoided."

"There won't be any complications. I'll make sure."

"I'll remind you of that," Cota said. "Down the road."

She parked behind the pickup, got out, left the motor running. An owl hooted from the treeline.

Chance came out the side door, a duffel bag slung over his shoulder. She opened the trunk. "How'd it go?"

"I said what I had to say. She did the same. I told her I'd call her tomorrow."

"Sorry."

He dropped the duffel in the trunk. She shut the lid.

"Nothing to be sorry about," he said. "It's done. Let's go."

ELEVEN

Three days later, they were at a motel in Boulder City, thirty miles from Las Vegas. It was old-style, attached cabins arranged in a U, just off a two-lane that had once been a main road.

She and Chance had rented adjoining cabins the day before, reserved another for the two men from Boston. They'd flown in that morning. Keegan was barrel-chested, with thinning red hair swept back, sideburns, and a broken nose. McBride, the one he'd brought in, was smaller, younger, dark-haired, and barely spoke at all.

The four of them sat around the table in Chance's cabin. McBride was biting his cuticles. His skin was pale, and he'd yet to make eye contact with her. She wondered how long he'd been out of prison.

"How about a beer?" Chance said. "Cut the dust."

"A grand idea," Keegan said. He had a soft Irish accent.

Chance got up, went into the kitchenette.

To Keegan, she said, "Sladden recommended you. Bobby did, too. That's why I asked you here."

He nodded.

"But I don't really know you," she said. "Or your partner here. So don't be offended if it takes a while to get things sorted out between us."

"Only natural," he said. "And the two of them said some fine things about your own self. That's why we came."

"I appreciate it."

"We have other mutual acquaintances, I'm sure, back east. There's a fellow named Smith, out of Pennsylvania, that worked with you once or twice, I believe."

"Smitty," she said. "How is he?"

"Above ground and walking free. All any of us can ask for, isn't it? I met your Mr. Boudreaux once as well, in St. Paul many years back. We were looking at some work there, but it never came to pass."

"Before my time," she said.

"It could be. Had a patch of bad luck himself recently, I heard."

"He did."

Chance came back in carrying open bottles of beer, set them on the table.

"Ah, Coors Light," Keegan said. "Like sex in a canoe."

"How's that?" Chance said.

"Fucking near water."

McBride laughed. Chance sat, said, "Sorry, I'll buy Guinness next time."

"Not on my account," Keegan said. "Never a favorite. Sacrilege, I know."

He looked at her. "These two we're waiting on, they're army?"

"Marines," she said. "Used to be."

McBride looked at her for the first time.

"Feckin' soldiers," he said. He turned to Keegan. "You didn't tell me that."

"Used to be," she said again. "Private now. They work for the man who's putting this together. He's paying them, but they answer to me."

"Sean's got a thing against soldiers," Keegan said. "British soldiers anyway. Hard to blame him. His uncle was murdered in cold blood on the Falls Road. Didn't even have a weapon on him. SAS. Bleeding assassins."

"Sorry to hear that," she said. McBride chewed a cuticle, said nothing.

"Well, it was all a long time ago, wasn't it?" Keegan said. "New life, new country. All the old sorrows left behind, right, Sean?"

"That's what they want," McBride said. "They want you to forget."

"Sometimes," she said, "that's not a bad thing."

Chance raised his bottle. *"Slainte."*

"Slainte," Keegan said. He and Chance clicked bottles. McBride lifted his and drank. She let hers sit.

They heard an engine outside, close by the door. She went to the front window, eased the curtain aside. A big Chevy SUV with smoked windows had parked next to her rental.

"They're here," she said.

When she opened the door, Hicks came in, smiled at her, said, "Hey." Behind him was a stocky, muscular Hispanic man in a tight V-necked T-shirt. He looked at her, then at the three men.

"This is Sandoval," Hicks said. "Sandy. One of my guys."

She shut the door behind them. Hicks nodded at the men. "Gents."

Keegan crossed his arms, nodded back. Chance lifted his bottle by the neck, raised his chin. McBride did nothing at all.

"Long ride," Sandoval said. "I need to take a leak."

Chance nodded down the hallway. Sandoval went past them. He was scouting, she knew, checking out the rest of the cabin.

To Hicks, Chance said, "Couple beers left in the fridge. Help yourself."

Hicks went into the kitchenette. When he came back out, a bottle in each hand, she said, "Everybody's up to speed. Mick and Sean got in today. We've covered the basics."

"Good," Hicks said. "Same here." They heard the toilet flush.

"Chairs over there," she said. "Go ahead and grab them."

Sandoval came back out. Hicks handed him a bottle, then dragged in two folding chairs from the other room, shook them open. He uncapped his beer, sat. Sandoval did the same.

"Okay," Hicks said. "What else can you tell us?"

"Bobby," she said, and he reached inside the jacket hanging on the back of his chair, took out the folded map. He spread it out on the table. With a grease pencil, she'd traced the stretch of highway she'd picked, marked X's for the location of the cell tower, the largest of the boulders, the arroyo that ran parallel to the roadway.

"Desert," Sandoval said. "No shit. That why I'm here?"

She looked at him.

"Because I'm Mexican, right?" he said. "You figure I know my way around there? That's a little racist, don't you think?"

"I had no idea what you were," she said. "Until you walked in that door."

"Don't pay any attention to him," Hicks said. "He's a smartass. You'll get used to it."

Sandoval grinned, drank beer.

She leaned over the map and traced a finger north along the highway.

"Hicks and I have been over this," she said. "But the rest of you need to know the setup. Three of you"—she pointed at Keegan, McBride, and Chance—"will be in a car hidden back in these hills. We'll have a truck stashed there, too, a clean one. We can talk about the division of labor later, but it'll be Bobby doing most of the driving. Hicks and Sandoval and I will be here"—she pointed at where the boulder was marked—"out of sight. That's where we'll stop the convoy. You three will come up the rear in the car. We get the guards and drivers under control, check the truck to make sure what we came for is in there. Then Bobby turns it around, drives it back to where the other truck's hidden, and the three of you transfer the cargo as quick as you can."

"Why not just bring the clean truck up in the first place?" Sandoval said. "Save some driving?"

"We don't want too many vehicles on the road at once," she said. "If we're all getting in each other's way, it raises the chances of something going wrong. This way's cleaner, simpler. Also, we don't know how long it'll take to transfer the cargo, even with forklifts. So it's better that's done out of sight, back up in those rocks. If we try to load up here, where we stopped them"—she touched the map—"it increases our exposure. Too many vehicles, too many people, too much time."

"What's the ground like back there?" Sandoval said. "Will it handle those trucks? You don't want them getting stuck."

She nodded at him. He was asking the right questions.

"Solid rock," she said. "I've already checked. Shouldn't be a problem with the truck, or the forklifts, getting stuck. After we load the clean truck, we camouflage the old one as best we can."

"Only five men to be dealt with," Keegan said. "We're sure of that?"

"If that changes, we'll know in advance," she said. "But we'll need to contain those five as quickly as possible. No fuss, no drama. We get them out of their vehicles and zip-tied quick as we can, move them behind the boulder, out of sight of the road. That way the area's clear if another car comes along before we're done."

"We'll have to move fast," Hicks said. "But dealing with civilians, that can be an issue."

"That'll be your job," she said. "Keep them calm, keep them quiet, but keep them scared."

"That's what you want the ordnance for," Sandoval said.

"Right," she said. "I don't want any of those five men even thinking about going cowboy. The guards will be armed, so they'll be the first priority. Handguns only, but still, we'll need to neutralize them as quickly as possible, get them disarmed and tied up. We get the guards under control, the civilians will follow."

"If we're lucky," Keegan said.

"We'll have speed on our side," she said. "By the time they realize what happened, we'll be out of there."

McBride leaned over, touched the map. "This mark here?"

"Cell tower," she said.

Keegan looked at her. "Is that a problem?"

"No," Hicks said. "I'll take care of that."

"Those people," Chance said. "We just leave them there?"

"When that tower goes off-line," she said, "it'll set off an alarm at the central office. They'll send somebody out quick. But as remote as this is, it'll take them at least twenty minutes, probably longer, to get there. They'll find the men. We'll be long gone."

She lifted her bottle, drank. The beer was cold and smooth, soothed her throat. She watched their faces, waiting for their response.

"Son of a bitch," Sandoval said, still looking at the map.

"We still have to gather all the equipment," she said to Hicks. "Your end."

"In a day or so, we'll have a house," he said. "Empty and out of sight, but room enough for everybody. We'll use that as our staging area. Everyone stays there. We run through the whole thing as many times as we have to, so everybody knows what they're doing. Come the day, we don't want anyone fucking around out there while the clock's ticking."

"If there's any fecking around," McBride said, "it won't be on our part. Know that."

Hicks looked at him. "Another country heard from."

"Rest assured," Keegan said. "That won't be an issue."

"Nothing personal," Hicks said. "I'm just saying."

"As am I," Keegan said.

"What about the money?" she said.

"He's working on that," Hicks said. "He'll have something for you soon. Next day or so."

"Sooner the better," Chance said. "We're running out of time."

Hicks looked at him. "I don't think you'll need to worry about that, slick."

"I'm not worried, *slick*," Chance said. "Like the Irishman says, you just keep up your part of the deal."

"I'll make sure everyone gets their money," she said. It was time to stop this before it went further. "Like I said, my responsibility."

Hicks drank beer, looked at Chance. He didn't look away.

"Let's wrap this up," she said. To Hicks, she said, "You have my new cell. Call me when the wire transfers go through."

"I will."

She looked around the table. "Anybody have any other questions need to be answered this minute?"

Keegan shook his head. McBride chewed a thumb.

"I'll be in touch tomorrow," Hicks said. He stood, put his half-empty bottle on the table. Sandoval did the same. As Hicks moved behind her, he brushed fingertips across her shoulder. She stiffened. Chance looked at her.

"Hang on," she said, and got to her feet. "I'll walk you out."

Outside in the sunlight, she said, "Hold up a minute."

Hicks unlocked the SUV with the remote, turned to her. "What is it?"

Sandoval looked at them, then opened the passenger door, climbed up into the seat, left the door open.

She kept her voice low. "Don't be playing any games here."

"What games?"

"You know what I'm talking about. I need you to be professional, with me and with them." She nodded at the cabin door.

"You think I haven't been?"

"Like I said on the phone, what happened between us is one thing. This, what's going on right here, is something else."

"You done?"

She took a step away, watched him. "Yeah, I'm done."

"Feel better?"

"That's got nothing to do with it."

"Whatever," he said, and started for the SUV again.

"Don't do anything stupid," she said to his back, "and fuck this up."

He turned back to her.

"Honey," he said. "I'm not the one we need to worry about."

TWELVE

The furnished house was twenty miles from Vegas, in a development of modest homes and cul-de-sacs. It was a bedroom community, all the houses built in the last ten years, but there were vacant lots on the block. Other houses were finished but unoccupied, manufacturer's stickers still on the windows.

She and Chance had their own rooms upstairs. Keegan and McBride shared one down the hall. Hicks and Sandoval slept on the ground floor, Hicks in a side bedroom, Sandoval on the couch.

The house gave them more room, more privacy, than a motel could offer. It had an oversized garage, and a big backyard with an in-ground pool, empty now, and a high wooden fence. At night, the city was a bright glow in the distance.

On the second day, Hicks called them into the dining room, set two heavy black tactical bags on the table.

"We should go over all this now," he said. "So you all know what you're dealing with when the time comes."

He unzipped the bags, began to lay weapons out on the table. Four short-barreled automatic rifles, three handguns, a silver and black riot shotgun. It was the first time she'd seen them. She was used to being in on every step of the planning, the financing, the equipment. But they were in Hicks's realm of expertise now. It was better for the job, better for the team, if she let him take the reins on what he knew best.

Sandoval looked at the guns, gave a low whistle. He wore a white strap T-shirt, a gold cross on a chain. On the back of his right shoulder was the same tattoo she'd seen on Hicks that night at the motel, a grinning skull, fangs.

The rifles were flat black, with curved magazines. She picked one up. It was lighter than she'd expected, with an adjustable stock and a knurled grip beneath the barrel that made it easier to handle.

"Sweet, isn't it?" Hicks said. "Heckler and Koch 416. It's what the SEAL teams use."

Guns meant little to her. They were just tools. "It's small."

"Yeah, it's a carbine model," he said. "Another miracle of German engineering. Like the Volvo."

"Volvos are Swedish," she said.

"Whatever. That switch right there is the safety. And the one on the side here is the magazine release. Twenty-round mag, five-five-six ammo. Round hits like a freight train, even with a suppressor cutting muzzle velocity."

McBride picked up another of the rifles, ejected the magazine. It was empty. He fit it back into the receiver, slapped it home, worked the bolt left-handed.

"Know how to handle one of those?" Hicks said.

"I've dabbled, now and then," McBride said. "At the range, you know."

"Paper targets don't shoot back."

"Neither do people," McBride said. "If you shoot them first."

Chance looked at Hicks, said, "You don't think we're going to need all these, do you?"

"No," Hicks said. "But I want you all to get familiar with them. When we're out there, everyone should look like they know what they're doing. Might be the difference between someone behaving, doing what they're told, and trying to rush you, thinking they can take your weapon away."

She stepped back from the table, lifted the rifle to her shoulder, tucked the butt in tight. Keegan looked amused.

"You wanted something that would intimidate," Hicks said. "That should do it."

"Intimidated a few *hajjis* back in the day," Sandoval said. "It's the conversation piece that ends the conversation."

"You can go ahead and adjust that stock," Hicks said. "Make it more comfortable."

"It's fine." She lowered the rifle. "What's this thing on top?" A small black cylinder was mounted over the barrel.

"Laser sight," Hicks said. "Can't really see it in the daytime, or I'd show you. But we're not going to need it anyway. Go ahead and clear the chamber, then drop the mag."

She did, slipped the safety on, put the rifle back on the table, the empty magazine beside it.

"How's it feel?" he said.

"Manageable. But like you said, it's the appearance that counts."

"The suppressors make them even scarier. People see those, they know you're not fucking around."

"As far as that," Keegan said, "I'll stay with what I know." He picked up the shotgun, looked it over.

"Remington 870," Hicks said. "Police tactical model. Work that pump and it gets people's attention. There's no other sound like it."

"I'm aware," Keegan said. He put the shotgun back down, picked up one of the automatics.

"I have suppressors for those as well," Hicks said. "And military slings for the rifles."

"What was it, Christmas?" Chance said. "Santa bring you all this shit?"

Hicks didn't smile. "Object is to get those people out of their vehicles and under control as quickly as possible. That's what the weapons are for. A deterrent."

"And what if they don't get out?" Chance said.

"We convince them they should. You were in the Corps, right? That what I hear?"

Chance looked at her, then back at Hicks. "Yeah."

"Then you know your way around ordnance."

"Some of it."

McBride said, "When do we get rounds?"

"Day of," Hicks said. "Still working on that part."

She said, "All of this gets dumped when we're finished, right?"

"Of course," Hicks said.

McBride thumbed the switch on the laser sight, and a faint red dot appeared on the wall, just to the left of the doorway. Chance took a step away from it.

"Like I said, can't really see it in daylight," Hicks said. "In the dark, though, it scares the shit out of people. Someone looks down, sees that little circle on their chest, they get compliant pretty quickly. It has what you'd call a powerful psychological effect."

"We'll want to lube the HKs a final time when we get out there," Sandoval said. "Especially with all that dust in the air."

"We going to steal some statues?" Chance said. "Or start a war?"

McBride turned off the laser, set the rifle back on the table.

"Either way, *ese*," Sandoval said, "we got you covered."

That afternoon, she took Chance out to the site. She had him drive, wanted him to learn the route.

When they came to the turnoff, she said, "Up there. It's safe. Just take it slow."

He steered the rental onto the dirt road and up the incline, pebbles rattling against the undercarriage. The road circled behind a cluster of rust-colored boulders and into a wide clearing, hemmed in by rocks on all sides, invisible from the highway.

"Where we'll stash the second truck," she said. "And where you, Keegan, and McBride will be waiting with the other car."

"Lucky me. Where exactly will you be?"

"With Hicks and Sandoval, just up the road."

"They like their guns, don't they, those two?"

"It's their livelihood," she said. "Let's go back out to the highway. I want to show you the rest."

He turned back down the road, the car rocking on the rugged ground. At the highway, he waited for a station wagon to pass, then bumped the car onto the blacktop, turned left.

"How much traffic on this road?" he said.

"Not a lot, but enough that we can't waste time. When we move, we have to move quick."

"Hit and git."

"That's right."

He picked up speed. Ahead, dust rose in the station wagon's wake. Heat created a shimmering water mirage on the roadway.

After a few minutes, she said, "Slow down. There, see the rock ahead, on the left? Pull over there."

He guided the car onto the right shoulder, slowed to a stop.

"Shut the engine off," she said. "Let's walk."

They got out, and he followed her across the road. The heat was oppressive. He got cigarettes from his pocket, lit one.

She showed him the depression behind the boulder. "Back here is where we'll be, and there"—she pointed out to the road—"is where we'll stop them."

"Got it." He looked around, squinted at the mountains. "Wide open around here."

"It is."

"I'm not used to working like this. Great outdoors and all that. Makes me a little nervous."

"This is the only way to do it. You having second thoughts?"

"I didn't say that."

"I've known you a long time, Bobby. If there's a problem, we need to talk about it."

He shrugged, flicked the half-smoked cigarette onto the ground.

"Don't leave that there," she said. "We don't want some CSI genius finding it afterward, your DNA all over it."

"Sorry." He bent, picked up the butt, snuffed it out with his fingers. "I don't know what I was thinking."

She watched him for a moment, then said, "Let's head back. I don't want to stand out here too long." He put the butt in his jeans pocket.

Back in the car, he started the engine, and she craned in her seat to look behind them, said, "It's clear." He made a wide U-turn onto the road, headed back the way they'd come.

"I talked to my guy in New York today," she said. "The front money came through."

Rathka had called her that morning to tell her the second transfer—a hundred and fifty thousand—had been wired to her account.

"Sladden'll handle mine," Chance said. "I talked to him already. He'll whack it up into seven or eight checks, mail them to Lynette."

"He'll take his cut first, of course."

"Yeah, but he's welcome to it. I haven't given him much work the last couple years. Never know when I'll need him again."

"He'll get a finder's fee from me, too, when we're done, for putting this together. And a percentage."

"All that," Chance said, "without ever having to leave his office. I want me one of those gigs." He got out his cigarettes again, said, "Mind?"

She shook her head. He lit one.

"Be straight with me," she said. "There some other issue I need to know about?"

He gave that a moment, said, "I don't know. There's something about all this. I keep thinking about Lynette, leaving her like I did. Wondering what'll happen to her if I don't get back."

"You'll get back."

"You say that, but no one knows for sure, do they? I mean, it's the nature of what we do. Uncertainty. Risk."

"Never bothered you before."

"I'm older now, I guess. With something to lose."

"You can walk," she said. "If that's what you want to do. I don't want you in this if your head's not in the right place. That's no good for any of us."

They passed the turnoff, drove on. She reached into the knapsack at her feet, took out a bottle of water, cracked it open and handed it to him, got one for herself.

"Thanks," he said, and snugged it between his legs.

"Listen," she said. "You don't have anything to prove, especially to me. You want to walk, it doesn't feel right to you, say the word. You don't need to explain yourself to anyone."

"No, I'm good. I'm not backing out."

"It's been a while since you worked."

"Yeah."

"And the last time you did you got hurt bad."

"That too."

"So it's only natural you'd be gun-shy, going out again for the first time. Like you said, you have things to lose now. Lynette. The farm."

"That's part of it."

"What's the other part?"

"This feels different. Like we're working for somebody."

"You are," she said. "You're working for me."

"That's not what I mean. It's like, usually, you go into something, whoever's running the crew is in charge, you know?

Whether it's you or Wayne or whoever. This feels like someone else's show."

"It's my show," she said. "At least this end. The financing, the equipment, all that, yeah, that's someone else's worry. But the way I look at it, that frees us up to concentrate on our part, eliminates some of the risks."

"Maybe. But that Hicks . . ."

"What about him?"

"I don't like the guy."

"You don't have to."

"Something about him."

"You only work with people you like?" Surprised to find herself defending Hicks, not sure why.

"He's not one of us."

"What's that?"

He looked at her. "A criminal."

"Don't be too sure."

"And I'm worried about what's going on between you two."

"What's that mean?"

"Nothing. Forget it."

She felt her face grow warm. "Speak your mind."

"The way he looks at you, I can tell. Way you look at him sometimes, too. Makes me wonder if there's something going on there."

"There isn't. And even if there was, how would that be different from when I worked with Wayne?"

"He's not Wayne."

She sat back, let her breath out slow.

"If you think I'm not up to running this," she said, "or that I've got things on my mind other than the work, then walk."

"Not what I meant."

"I need you, but I'll do this without you if I have to. In or out. Make up your mind." Regretting it as soon as she said it.

He looked at her again. "I said I'm in."

"Good. Then get your head straight. We've got a lot of work ahead."

"What I'm here for," he said.

THIRTEEN

Sandoval cooked for them that night, chorizo and chopped potatoes with onions, the smell of it filling the house. They ate separately, he and Hicks in the kitchen, Keegan and McBride in the room they shared upstairs. She and Chance were in the dining room, at the table where the guns had been. On the wall were maps, and the photos she'd taken of the site.

"How's Lynette?" she said. He'd called her from his cell as soon as they'd gotten back to the house.

"She's all right. Freaks her out a little, being home all alone. Still a little pissed at me, too."

"Sorry."

"Not your fault. And you're right about those two." He nodded toward the kitchen. "They know their business. I just need to concentrate on my part."

"You'll be fine. Get behind the wheel again, it'll feel like old days."

"That's what I'm worried about. I get started again, I might not want to stop."

"You can always stop."

"Can you?"

She let that pass, said, "She know the money's coming?"

"I told her. It'll help. She knows it's cash that makes it all happen. She may not like how I made it, but she'll be happy I did."

She gestured toward the stairs. "What do you know about this McBride?"

"Not a lot. Way he talks, I'm guessing he was a baby provo back in his teenage days. Probably here illegally. Fugitive, maybe. Either way, Keegan trusts him. And I trust Keegan, far as it goes."

"You two go back?"

"Just to that Rhode Island thing. Bread truck takedown, with a good pull. But his reputation preceded him."

"What's that mean?"

"He's a real OG, goes all the way back to Whitey Bulger's crew, that Winter Hill mob in Boston in the seventies. He mostly took down scores, but word is he also whacked two Italians who were giving Whitey grief. Plus another guy that was helping Whitey run guns to the IRA. Whitey took the money for the guns, then sold out all his partners to the FBI. All except for Keegan. Too scared of him to take the chance, I guess."

Hicks rapped on the door frame, then came into the room. They turned to him. He held three bottles of Corona by their necks. "Beers?"

"Sure," Chance said.

Hicks put the sweating bottles on the table, pulled up a chair. "How's it looking on your end?"

"Fine," she said. "We were out there today. No hitches. It should work the way we planned it."

"Good." He looked at Chance. "You agree?"

"Yeah," Chance said. "As long as everyone does their part."

"They will, I'm sure," Hicks said. He lifted his bottle. "To the work." He looked at her. "That's what you call it, right? It's all just work."

She didn't answer. Chance lifted his bottle and drank. Hicks did the same. She left hers where it was. In the kitchen, Sandoval was singing softly in Spanish. They could hear the clatter of dishes in the sink.

Chance stood. "I'm going to go outside and have a cigarette. Thank your buddy for the food."

He took his bottle with him. They heard the front door open and close.

"He going to be a problem?" Hicks said.

"What's that mean?"

"Just wondering."

"No, he isn't. Are you?"

He smiled. "No. But I owe you an apology for the other day, at the motel."

"Forget it."

"No, you're right. I was out of line."

She looked at him, wanting to be done with it. "It's like you said, this is work. There are enough ways to screw it up already. We don't need to create any more."

"I know," he said.

"A few days from now, we'll all go our separate ways, maybe never see each other again. But until then, we're a team. We need to act like one. That means everything else gets left at the door."

"You're right. And I'll keep that in mind from now on."

"Tell your partner, too."

"Sandy's a pro. He knows all that already. Maybe better than me. I let some personal things get in the way. It's not like me."

"Glad to hear it."

"What about your guys?"

"They know what they need to do."

"Not many laughs in that bunch. And I don't think they like me very much."

"It is what it is."

"Too bad."

"We just have to work together," she said. "We don't have to be friends. You hear from Cota today?"

"Yeah. Everything's on schedule. He made the transfer. The other truck's ready, too. Sandy and I will pick it up tomorrow night, drive it here, park it in the garage. Then we can practice with the lifts, getting the doors open, all of that. A few days and we should be good."

Five days to go before the work. It couldn't come soon enough for her. With men cooped up like this, waiting, nervous, there was always the risk of trouble.

"Night before, Sandy or me will drive the truck out to the site, camo it," he said. "One of us will follow, take the other back. Your guys don't need to be involved."

"What about the other vehicles?"

"There's a long-term lot out by the airport, privately run. I have a guy there. We'll go the day before, get what we need, ditch them when we're done."

"Then that's that," she said.

He lifted his beer.

"Then here's to the mission," he said. "Everybody goes home."

When she went up to their room, Keegan and McBride had finished eating, were playing cards at a table by the window, money in front of them, along with a bottle of Jameson and two glasses. She wondered where they'd gotten it, if they'd brought it with them. Hoped the drinking wouldn't become a problem.

"Your money's in," she said. Keegan had given her his account information the day before, and Rathka had put through the transfer directly, along with McBride's share.

"So it is," Keegan said. "I made a call earlier, and was told the same. On its way to Costa Rica as we speak. Or perhaps one of those other countries in that part of the world. I often forget which."

She looked at McBride. "What about yours?"

Keegan said, "I believe Sean, for his own purposes, always prefers his end in hard currency. We'll work that out between us."

"That's a lot of cash," she said to McBride. "You'll need to be careful what you do with it."

"I will be," McBride said.

Keegan put his cards facedown on the table. "Calls for a bit of a celebration, don't you think? There's another glass on the dresser there."

"No, thanks."

"You won't have one with us?" McBride said, looking at her for the first time.

"There'll be plenty of time after to celebrate," she said. "There's still a lot of work to do."

"Have no bother on that account," Keegan said. "Just killing time, aren't we? It's the waiting that's the weary part."

"I know," she said, backing off, keeping the peace. "We'll have the truck tomorrow. Then more details to go over."

"Ah, the details," Keegan said. "And that selfsame devil that goes along with them. Isn't that the holy all of it."

FOURTEEN

They spent the final days working with the truck, going over the materials, familiarizing themselves with the weapons. It kept everyone busy, focused.

The truck matched the one she'd seen in the pictures at Cota's house. It was about twelve feet high, fifteen feet long, dirty white. They'd backed it into the garage, and Sandoval had used stencils and spray paint to print ALMAREYDA SEAFOOD LAS VEGAS/ RENO on its side.

On the last day, she went out to the garage, found Hicks and Sandoval standing at the workbench that ran along one wall. They wore latex gloves. Chance was leaning back against the front fender of the truck, watching them.

She came up behind Hicks. On the workbench were four small blocks of what looked like bright white clay, laid out on thick waxed paper.

"What's this?" she said.

"What we've been waiting for." Using a plastic knife, he cut a block into two pieces.

"Is that safe?" she said.

"C-4's stable," Hicks said. "Inert without a detonator. It'll burn, but it won't explode. In Nam, grunts used it to cook. They'd fire up a little piece, heat their rations."

"Where are the detonators?"

"Over there." On the bench a few feet away was a gray plastic case the size of a cigarette pack. "They don't get near each other until game time."

"How will you set them off?"

"Remote control triggers. Basically radio transmitters set to a certain frequency. I have those already as well. We're all set on this front."

"That's good to hear."

"Trust me," he said. "Everything's under control."

She woke with a start. The room was dark, moonlight slanting across the bed. In the quiet of the house, she could hear Sandoval's faint snoring downstairs.

She got out of bed, took her watch from the nightstand—three A.M. She needed sleep, but the nights before work were almost always a lost cause. Lack of rest could catch up with her, she knew, impair her judgment, slow her reflexes. But there was nothing for it. The adrenaline was already starting to work in her, her mind buzzing over last-minute details, possibilities.

Earlier that night, Sandoval had driven the truck out to the turnoff, stowed it up in the rocks. Hicks had driven him back in the black Jeep Cherokee he'd stolen from the airport lot. Now the

Cherokee and the second car they'd taken, a nondescript Ford Focus, were parked in the garage. She'd left her own rental two blocks away.

At the window, she looked out on the backyard. The moon was almost full, lit the snowy peaks in the distance.

She pulled on jeans and a sweater, slipped bare feet into sneakers. Wide awake now, and no use fighting it. She went quietly into the carpeted hall and down the stairs. Sandoval was snoring deeply in the living room. Hicks's door was closed.

Out through the sunporch and onto the patio. The night was chill. Stars stretched across the clear sky.

There were folding canvas chairs leaning against the wall. She opened one, the aluminum frame cold to the touch, set it by the empty pool.

She sat and looked off at the mountains, thought about the distance, the vast stretch of emptiness that began where this development ended. Thought about Wayne in his six-by-ten cell. How the odds were he'd never see open land like this again in his life.

The porch door squeaked behind her. She turned to see Hicks in the doorway. He wore jeans, a black sleeveless T-shirt.

"Couldn't sleep," he said. "Heard you moving around out here. Mind if I sit?"

She shook her head, looked off at the mountains again. He came out, eased the door shut behind him, rubbed his arms. He was barefoot.

"You must be freezing out here," he said.

"I'm all right."

He sank down on the concrete beside her, sat cross-legged. "Not long now."

"No," she said. "You talk to Cota? Tell him we're on schedule?"

"Called him tonight. He was somewhat reassured. But he's a very careful and paranoid old man. He won't relax until those things are on their way across the ocean and he's got the rest of his money."

A coyote howled somewhere. She remembered what Cota had told her back in Los Angeles.

"Maybe not so paranoid," she said. "He's running a lot of risks."

"Calculated risks. The only kind he takes. He'll clear a bundle from this, and not just what he'll get from the buyer."

She looked at him. "What do you mean?"

"What do you think? On one level, the whole thing's a scam. After he acknowledged he owned those pieces—if not so much how he got them—he had them appraised for twice their actual value, by a guy he had in his pocket. Then he insured them for the inflated value. When they're stolen, he'll file a claim. So he walks away with the money from his buyer, under the table, and collects the insurance as well."

"He should have told me."

"I guess he saw it as a need-to-know situation."

"Insurance claims mean insurance investigators," she said. "They'll be out there at the site afterward, taking pictures, measuring skid marks. There's no way around that. But if they start to suspect fraud, they'll be all over him as well, poking into his business, finding out who he was talking to, what he was doing, in the days leading up to it. They'll put pressure on the appraiser, too."

"Maybe, maybe not. What could they prove anyway? Likely nothing. As far as he's concerned, it's worth the risk."

"That supposed to make me feel better?"

"What you have to understand about him"—he touched his

temple—"is he's always thinking five moves ahead. It's his gift. It's how he got where he is."

"Along with having you to watch his back?"

"I guess I come in handy sometimes. My skill set, that is."

"A gun for hire?"

"That still bother you? Like I said, when it comes down to it, are we so different, you and me? We do what we do. More importantly, we do what we *have* to do, to get things accomplished. At least we're honest about it, right? You know what they say: to live outside society, you must have a code."

"That's a joke, right?"

"Maybe not."

"What's your code?"

The howling came again.

"Take care of my partners," he said. "Do what I'm paid to do. Do what it takes."

He stood without using his hands, stretched. She felt him move behind her, then his hands were on her shoulders, gentle but firm. He began to knead the muscles there, press his thumbs into the knotted tension in the back of her neck. She closed her eyes, felt a slow release as the tendons relaxed. He put his left palm on her forehead, gently guided her head back while his right hand worked at her neck.

She started to give in to the gentle pressure, and then suddenly it all felt wrong. She opened her eyes, stiffened, and he felt the resistance there, stopped what he was doing. He let his hands rest on her shoulders. She hunched, and he took them away.

"Sorry," he said.

She rolled her shoulders. They were looser now. She looked back at him. "We've got work."

"I know."

"Maybe afterward." Lying.

"Yeah, right."

"You should get some rest. We've got a long day tomorrow."

He turned and went back inside without a word. She listened until the sound of his footsteps was gone, then turned back to the night and the moon.

FIFTEEN

The vultures were just black specks at first, outlined against the low sun. Through the binoculars, she watched them glide lazily on the thermal currents, three of them now. They began to make long slow circles far above.

"*Zopilotes*," Sandoval said behind her. "When I was a kid, sometimes me and my sister, we'd mess with them." She lowered the binoculars, looked at him. He was in the passenger seat of the Cherokee, door open, an HK across his lap. He was using a cloth to wipe it down.

"We'd go out in the desert, lie flat and just wait," he said. "It wouldn't take long. Ten, fifteen minutes. We'd see 'em way up high at first. Then they'd come down, check us out. The trick was not to move. Then, when they were like five feet above us, ready for that first taste, we'd jump up and yell. They'd fly away twice as fast. It was fun, you know? Fucking with the *carroñeros*."

The Cherokee was parked in the shadow of the boulder. Hicks

was up on the road, kneeling on the blacktop, an entrenching tool and a now-silent blowtorch beside him. He'd used the blowtorch to soften a section of the roadway, and the smell of hot tar was in the air.

He and Sandoval wore desert camo jumpsuits zipped high over Kevlar vests, loose green army surplus scarves looped around their necks. She wore a black jumpsuit over street clothes, work boots. They hadn't offered her a vest, and she hadn't asked.

"Down by the border, though," Sandoval said, "they get their share of human meat. All those *mojados* who try to come across and don't make it. They die from thirst or hunger, sunstroke, freeze to death at night. Sometimes the coyotes they pay to take them across just leave them out there in the desert. If they don't shoot them first, rape the women. The birds eat well then. They get a taste for it."

To the north, a dust cloud on the road. "Car," she said.

Hicks got up, brushed himself off, went to the Cherokee and opened the rear hatch, put the blowtorch and e-tool inside. He pulled up on his gloves to tighten them. "We're good."

"You looked like you knew what you were doing out there," she said.

"Let's hope."

A vehicle materialized out of the heat shimmer. She moved back farther behind the boulder. A minivan blew by without slowing, left dust in the air.

When it was out of sight, Hicks took a pair of bolt cutters and a black utility bag from the Cherokee, started toward the cell tower. She followed.

Usually, just before the actual work, she was calm, steady. But now she felt a vague anxiousness, thinking of a dozen ways things could go wrong. She'd had to trust others more this time, give up control of certain elements, things she was used to handling herself. She knew it was for the best, but it still left her uneasy.

When they got to the chain-link fence around the equipment compound, she said, "You sure this isn't electrified?"

"We're about to find out."

"Not funny."

"I'm sure. If it was, there'd be insulators every few feet, ground wires. I don't see any."

He nodded at the fence. She gripped a section of the chain-link with her thin leather gloves, held it taut while he used the bolt cutters to snap through links, starting at the bottom. Halfway up, he stopped, wiped sweat from his forehead. She gripped the fence higher, feeling the slack in it now. He cut through links up to head height, then across. When he was done, he set the bolt cutters down, and together they bent the flap of fence out and back onto itself, hooked it there. He carried the utility bag inside.

The phone in her side pocket began to buzz. It was one of a set of disposables she'd bought the day before. They each had one.

"We're on it," Chance said. "Just passed the mile marker here. As advertised." Meaning the convoy was on its way, the number of vehicles as expected.

"Anything between you and the follow car?" she said.

"Nothing. We're a ways back, so someone else might get in there. But I'll deal with it if it happens."

Hicks had the utility bag open, was kneeling beside a thick silver pipe that ran from one equipment cabinet to another.

"ETA?" she said.

"Thirty minutes," Chance said. "I'll call back in fifteen. We're all set here." He ended the call.

Hicks looked back at her.

"Thirty minutes," she said.

"Plenty of time."

She put the cell away, watched him. He'd already molded a piece of C-4 around the pipe, was fitting a silver tube into the center of it. When he was done, he shaped another piece around a second pipe that right-angled from a low metal box. The humming was loud here, the feeling of electricity in the air.

"No chance someone gets on the wrong frequency by accident?" she said. "Radio-controlled airplane or something? Detonates that before we're ready?"

"Unlikely, all the way out here." He grinned up at her. "But if you see one flying around, shout."

"You're enjoying this, aren't you?"

"A little. But at some point you have to stop worrying and trust your equipment. These detonators only work on a dedicated frequency, and that's keyed to the trigger mechs I brought. Trust me, it'll be fine. We're done here."

He rose, zipped up the utility bag and slung it over his shoulder. When he came through the fence, she pulled the chain-link flap free and let it sag back into place. They walked back to the Cherokee.

Sandoval was standing outside the open rear passenger door, the duffel bag of weapons on the seat. He took out a suppressor, began to thread it into the muzzle of his HK. Hicks was right, it made the gun look even more threatening, more deadly.

"You got enough joy juice on that thing?" Sandoval said. He took out a full magazine, rapped it against his knee, then fit it into place in the rifle, pushed it home.

"All we need," Hicks said. "Just a kiss. It'll do the job."

"Happy to see you still got the touch, homes." He worked the bolt to chamber a round, put the safety on.

Hicks set the utility bag in the back of the Cherokee, went around and got a black leather case from the glove box, unzipped it. "Have a look," he said to her.

Inside were two small olive-drab boxes with toggle switches on the front, red buttons on the sides. He took out one box, thumbed the toggle. A green light began to glow above it.

"This one's for the tower charges," he said. "Come the time, you want to do the honors?"

She shook her head. "Tell me again how it's going to work on the road."

"Just like I said. The space I hollowed out is only about ten inches deep, but when the charge goes off, it'll activate the black powder in there as well. Way I planned it, we should get a little pop, then smoke will start pouring out like the blacktop's on fire. Won't damage the road too much, but it'll make them stop."

"Will all the charges go at the same time?"

"No. Different frequencies, and I have to manually trigger both. The two in the tower will go first, but that's good. They see the smoke from that, it might slow them down before the road charge detonates. And that way we knock out their cells first thing. They'll be confused, and that's better for us. It'll make them easier to handle."

The sun was sinking behind the mountains, the Cherokee falling deeper into shadow. Sandoval took balaclavas from the weapons bag, tossed one to Hicks, then another to her. She caught it.

Her cell buzzed again.

"Fifteen," Chance said. "Car got between us, but then the

convoy slowed, so it passed. You'll be seeing that one soon, blue Chevy Capri. Nothing else in front of us."

"You three all set?"

"Good as we're gonna be."

"Last call unless there's an emergency," she said.

"Right. See you when we get there."

She put the phone away. Hicks and Sandoval were watching her, their balaclavas on, two masked figures in the desert twilight.

"Get ready," she said.

From here, just heat shimmer, dust. She focused the binoculars, and now she could see the lead car, a black Crown Victoria. Behind it, maybe two car lengths, was the truck.

"Here they come," she said.

There was a slight curve in the road up there, and when they hit it, she could see all three vehicles. The follow car, another black Crown Vic, was keeping the same distance. A half mile behind it was another dust cloud. Chance and the others.

Hicks had taken two HKs from the duffel bag, fit in suppressors, set the rifles on the roof of the Cherokee, in easy reach. Sandoval stood with his at port arms, his jaws moving beneath the balaclava. He was chewing gum.

She put the binoculars on the front seat, pulled at the chin of the balaclava to adjust it, then flexed her fingers to tighten the gloves. Hicks stood by the front of the Cherokee, watching the road. The two detonator switches were laid out on the hood.

"You ready?" she said.

"As ever."

She took down one of the rifles, checked to make sure the

safety was on. She saw him flick one toggle switch, then the other. Green lights glowed on both boxes.

She moved close to the Cherokee, out of sight of the road. The sound of tires on blacktop grew louder, closer. He looked at her, and she nodded.

He picked up one of the boxes, said, "Fire in the hole," and pressed the red button.

Two loud cracks, and puffs of white smoke billowed up over the equipment compound. Bits of metal rained down, and then the smoke drifted higher, dissipated in the wind.

She turned just in time to see the road charge go off. Another crack, not as loud, and a cloud of dust and smoke shot up out of the road, ten feet high, then seemed to spread and solidify, hang suspended in the air.

The lead car braked, swerved and went into a skid, passed sideways through the black cloud, rocked to a stop. A scream of brakes as the truck stopped behind it, and then the rear car thumped into the truck from behind, the grille and headlights crunching as they met the truck's loading deck. The Taurus came up behind it, braked to a stop.

She ran into the dust and smoke, reached the lead car, saw the two men inside, their stunned faces. She aimed the HK at the windshield, shouted, "Get out! Get out now!"

When they didn't move, she grabbed the latch on the driver's side door, pulled. It was unlocked, and as it came open she nearly lost her balance, stumbled back. The driver was in his thirties, balding with blond hair, wearing street clothes and a dark zippered jacket over a white shirt. The man beside him was in a blue uniform with yellow shoulder patches that said SECURITY. He was younger, skinny.

She steadied herself, aimed the HK at the driver, yelled, "Both of you! Out now, on the ground!"

The driver raised his hands. She moved toward him to reach in, grab his jacket, but he swung his legs out of the car, said, "Wait a minute, wait a minute." She stepped back to give him room. There was shouting all around her now.

"On the ground," she said again. "Both of you."

The guard came out after him, on the same side, hands in the air. He was a kid, in his twenties maybe, the uniform hanging loose on him. He wore a dark automatic in a hip holster.

"Facedown on the road, right there," she said. "Now."

The driver knelt, put his hands behind his head without being told. "You, too," she told the guard, and he looked around, confused. She pointed the HK at his chest.

"Down," she said.

He looked at her, then sank to his knees.

"Flat," she said, and they both stretched out on the roadway. She slung the HK behind her, plucked the guard's gun from his holster, pushed it into a jumpsuit pocket. She got out a pair of flexcuffs, knelt on the small of his back. "Take it easy," she said. "Relax, and no one gets hurt."

He flinched as she pulled his left arm behind him, then his right, bound his wrists with the flexcuffs, cinched them tight.

The driver had his head turned to the side, watching her. He'd already crossed his hands behind him, not waiting for the command. She flexcuffed his wrists, patted them both down for other weapons, found none.

"Stay there, "she said. The smoke was gone, but the acrid smell of it hung in the air. Where the charge had gone off was a hole about a foot across, a thin tendril of smoke rising from it. It had worked as Hicks said it would.

The driver was still in the truck. Sandoval stood on the running board, shouting at him, banging the butt of his HK against the window. The rear Crown Vic was already empty, both front doors open. The driver and guard, hands bound, were being led away by McBride and Keegan, both in balaclavas. Keegan had his shotgun against the back of the guard's head.

A masked figure came up beside her. Hicks. She pointed at the men on the ground, said, "Get them," and started toward the truck. Sandoval was still shouting at the driver. The window had spiderwebbed but was intact, the driver fumbling with a cell phone.

With the HK still slung behind her, she sprinted, planted a foot on the truck's front bumper, vaulted onto the hood, knelt there. The driver looked at her through the windshield, and she drew the guard's gun, fired a shot into the air. The casing clattered on the hood. She lowered the gun, pointed it at the driver, the muzzle touching the glass.

He punched numbers into the phone, panicking, and she gripped her right wrist with her left hand, steadied the gun, tapped the barrel twice on the windshield. He looked into the muzzle, exhaled, then tossed the cell phone onto the dashboard in disgust. She heard the click as he unlocked the door.

She slid down off the hood. When the driver started to get out, Sandoval caught his jacket, dragged him down, and kicked his legs out from under him. He fell to his knees, and Sandoval said, "Smart guy, huh?" and drove the butt of his HK into the side of the driver's head, knocked him down onto the road. He tried to crawl away, and Sandoval kicked him hard in the side with a booted foot.

"Stop it," she said. Sandoval looked at her, anger in his eyes.

"Get him tied and out of sight," she said. "We need to clear this road."

She didn't wait for a response, ran back to the lead car, the door still open, engine running. She tossed the HK onto the seat, pulled the door shut, slammed the shifter into drive. Giving it gas, she straightened the wheels, pulled onto the shoulder and drove twenty feet, then cut the wheel hard so the two front tires hung off the edge of the road, the hood tilting down into the arroyo. She shifted into neutral, then killed the engine, grabbed the HK, and got out.

When she looked back, they'd pushed the second Crown Vic to the side of the road, and Chance and McBride were at the back of the truck, working at the heavy padlock with a sledgehammer, Hicks watching them. Keegan and Sandoval had taken the rest of the men behind the boulder.

She went around to the rear of the first car. With her back to it, she gripped the bumper, pushed with hips and heels. The car creaked, protested, then began to roll, got away from her. She caught her balance, turned to see it head nosedown into the arroyo, in slow motion at first, then all at once. It overturned, landed on its roof, glass exploding, then slid down the side of the arroyo to the bottom, dust rising up. She tossed the guard's gun down after it.

Almost dark. She heard the truck's rear door go up on its rollers, ran back toward the others. Hicks and Chance clambered up onto the tailgate lift and into the bed. McBride stood on the shoulder, looking in both directions, his HK at ready.

At the truck, she climbed up into the driver's seat, took the cell phone from the dashboard. The screen read SEARCHING FOR SERVICE. She pulled her own phone from her pocket. It read the same.

The engine was off, but the keys were still in the ignition. She started the engine to save them a few seconds, then climbed down, lobbed the driver's cell phone out into the arroyo.

Hicks and Chance were up in the darkness of the truck bed, flashlights on. In their light, she saw three heavy crates bound to the far wall with bungee cords, sandbags laid at their base. The *lamassu*. There was another crate beside it, a quarter of the size, secured the same way. Then a fifth, smaller than the rest.

Hicks stood by the larger crates, playing his light up and down them. He knelt to inspect the others, then turned and jumped down from the truck bed. "Everything's here. We're good."

Chance climbed down after him. To McBride, she said, "You two go. We're clear." He jogged back toward the Taurus.

Chance reached up, caught the handle on the door, pulled. It came down loudly on its rollers, slammed into place. He threw the crossbar.

Hicks had the other Crown Vic in neutral, was pushing it back again, holding the wheel through the open driver's side window. She ran to help him, shoved on the front left fender, avoiding the jagged metal of the shattered grille. The rear tires went off the edge of the road, and he stepped clear as the car slid backward into the arroyo, the hood pointing up at the sky for a moment, then dropping down out of sight. She heard metal crunch as the car went down.

"I'm gone," Chance said. He climbed up into the truck cab. McBride and Keegan were already back in the Taurus, balaclavas off, Keegan driving. He pulled onto the shoulder, then made a long turn to swing around, head back the way they'd come.

She heard the truck's gears grind, stepped away. Chance steered to the left, using the big side mirror for guidance, negotiated a three-point turn. He pulled off his balaclava, lifted a hand to her as he drove past. The truck rumbled off in the Taurus's wake.

It was over. The road was clear. The only shot fired had been hers.

Dark now. Behind the boulder, Sandoval had all five men on their knees, facing the stone, hands bound. The Cherokee's engine was running, headlights on. Hicks was storing the last of their equipment in the back. The other three had left their weapons with him. Sandoval stood behind the men, his HK at port arms, still chewing gum.

The older of the two guards, gray hair in a military cut, uniform smeared with red dust, craned his neck to look behind him.

"You know what's in that truck?" he said. "It's not what you think. It won't be any use to you."

"Don't you worry about it," Sandoval said, and flicked the guard's ear with the HK's suppressor.

The guard twisted his head away as if in annoyance, looked back at him. "You ever use that weapon? Man to man? Shooting at someone who's shooting back?"

"Shut up," one of the men said. It was the driver of the truck. He was bleeding from a cut on his forehead. "Just do what they say."

"They're not gonna hurt us," the guard said. "They aren't killers. They're punks."

Sandoval laughed, came closer and slammed the butt of the

HK into the guard's shoulder. He grunted, fell facedown in the dirt. Sandoval put a boot on the back of his neck, held him there. "You should listen to your friend."

"Enough," she said. Sandoval looked at her, then took his boot away, stepped back.

The guard coughed and struggled back to his knees, trying to catch his breath, looking at the ground now. The other four were watching him. The driver she'd taken out of the first car was breathing shallow and fast, his face shiny with sweat.

"What's your name?" she said to him.

He closed his eyes, swallowed, then looked back at her. "It's okay. I'm with you. Everything's okay."

She frowned, wondering what that meant.

"Your name," she said.

"Why?"

"Answer her," Sandoval said.

She felt Hicks come up alongside her.

The driver turned his face away. He was starting to hyperventilate. "Charles."

"Charles what?"

"Conlon. You're going to kill us, aren't you?" His breathing was ragged, his shoulders trembling.

"Listen to me, Charles," she said. "You're all going to be okay."

He had his eyes shut tight again, and there were tears coming out from under them.

"All of you, listen," she said. "Before long, someone's going to be out here looking for you. A half hour tops, probably less. Either way, you'll all be fine. Later tonight you'll be telling this story to your wives and girlfriends. Don't give us any trouble, stay calm, and everybody gets to go home."

The gray-haired guard turned to look at her. There was blood on his lips. "How far do you think you'll get before that truck's spotted?"

"For Christ's sake, shut up," the truck driver said.

Conlon was shaking now. She turned to Hicks. "We need to get going."

He nodded, but didn't move. His HK hung from its sling, muzzle down. He had one hand on the butt.

Sandoval looked at him, said, "Well, *jefe*?"

Hicks looked down at the kneeling men. "What she said."

Sandoval said, "You sure?"

"Yeah. Let's move."

She went to the back of the Cherokee, unslung her HK, slid it into the tac bag there.

Hicks came up behind her, took off his rifle, said, "Better check the road."

She went out to the highway. Taillights in the distance. The Taurus and the truck. She watched as they grew dimmer, vanished. Nothing in the other direction.

There was the sound of a scuffle behind her. She turned fast, heard Hicks say, "No!" Then a figure came out from behind the boulder, running, hands bound behind him. Conlon.

She angled to cut him off. He slammed into her, and they both went down on the blacktop. He was panting as he rolled away, tried to get back to his feet. She kicked at his legs to trip him, missed, and then he was up and running again, down the center of the road, his gait awkward, the bound hands throwing him off balance.

He yelled, "Help! Somebody help us!" and Sandoval stepped

out from behind the boulder, said calmly, "Stop." A beam of red light bisected the darkness, shone on the running man's back.

"No!" she said, and rolled to her feet. "Charles! Stop!"

He turned toward her, stumbling, backpedaled. A red dot centered on his chest; then came the clack and snap of a rifle bolt. He spun around, legs tangled, fell face first onto the road.

She ran toward him, heard feet behind her. She reached Conlon, knelt beside him. He lay with his right cheek on the blacktop, eyes open. Hicks knelt next to her, said, "Goddamn it."

She tried to turn Conlon over, saw the blood soaking through his white shirt. She pulled off her left glove, touched her middle finger to his carotid artery, trying to feel a pulse beneath the skin. She tried another spot on his neck, an inch lower. Nothing.

"What?" Hicks said.

She sat back on her haunches. "He's dead."

"You sure?"

"Yes."

Sandoval stood on the shoulder, watching them. He'd turned off the laser sight.

"What happened?" she said.

"He got up, took a runner," Hicks said. "I told him to stop."

She pulled her glove back on, feeling the anger. Taking dirt from the road, she rubbed it against the spot where she'd touched him. It would cover any fingerprint or DNA she might have left.

"We were almost out of here," she said.

"I don't know what got into him. He just panicked, ran."

"We have to get him off the road. Help me."

They gripped his bound arms, rose. He was dead weight between them.

"Careful," Hicks said. "The blood."

They half carried, half dragged him across the road, his shoes scuffing on the blacktop.

"You shouldn't have let this happen," she said.

"He shouldn't have run."

"They were your responsibility."

Sandoval was back behind the boulder now, shouting at the others to stay where they were.

They laid Conlon alongside the Cherokee, out of sight of the men. She and Hicks were both out of breath.

"You bastards," the older guard said. "You murdering bastards."

"Shut up," Sandoval said. "I won't tell you again, *papi*."

She went around to the front of the Cherokee. Bugs flittered in the headlights. She looked at Sandoval. He had the butt of the HK braced on his hip.

"I told him to stop," he said. "Everyone heard me. He should have stopped. He didn't. What was I supposed to do?"

The skinny guard she'd taken from the first car had his eyes closed, was mumbling to himself, the cadences of prayer.

"We have to go," Hicks said.

"Just drive away," the truck driver said without turning. There was rising panic in his voice. "Leave us here. Just drive away. You got what you want."

"Be cool," Sandoval said to him. "Just stay where you are. Everything's gonna be all right."

Hicks looked at her. "We don't have a lot of choice here."

"No," she said, knowing what he meant.

The other guard had gone silent for a moment, was praying again. The Hail Mary.

"Wait a minute," she said. "Let's all just take a breath here."

Sandoval had moved to stand behind the older guard. He popped his gum, looked at Hicks. "Your call, *jefe*."

She took a step closer to the Cherokee, the rear hatch still open. Wondering how long it would take her to get the HK out, if the safety was on.

"No," she said again.

Hicks looked at her, then turned back to Sandoval, nodded.

"Wait," she said, and then Sandoval lowered the HK and shot the guard in the back of the head. Blood sprayed the boulder.

Beside him, the truck driver screamed, threw himself to the side. Sandoval took a step back, aiming now, fired three more times, the only sound the clack of the rifle bolt, the grunts of the men. Then all four were facedown in the dirt, gray gunsmoke drifting through the headlights.

She felt dizzy, the earth tilting under her feet. She reached the Cherokee, grabbed for the HK. Hicks drove a shoulder into her, knocked her away. She caught her balance, spun to face him, and then a red laser sight touched the center of her chest. Sandoval had the HK to his shoulder, finger on the trigger.

Hicks took a step away, said, "Hold on now. Everybody just hold the fuck on."

She looked at Sandoval. The laser was steady. She wondered what she would see when he fired. If she'd see anything at all.

A low moan came from one of the men on the ground.

Hicks looked at her, said, "It was the only way."

The red dot climbed her chest, blinded her for a moment, centered on her forehead. She held her breath.

Hicks said, "He'll do it, you know. If you make him."

152 | Wallace Stroby

The laser traced its way back down her body, hovered over where her heart would be.

"Sandy," Hicks said. "Ease up. It's okay."

"You sure of that, man?"

"I am."

Sandoval lowered the rifle. The red dot trailed down her leg and into the dirt at her feet.

Another moan. The skinny guard's right foot began to scuff softly at the dirt.

"Sandy," Hicks said.

Sandoval shook his head. "It can't be just me, man."

Hicks looked at him for a moment, then reached into the back of the Cherokee, took a dark automatic from the tac bag, a suppressor already threaded into the muzzle. He worked the slide.

"Don't," she said. Her mouth was dry.

"It's the only way," he said again, then walked over to the men, leaned over and carefully shot each of them in the head.

The night was silent again, except for the chugging of the Cherokee's engine. She couldn't breathe.

Hicks pulled off his balaclava. His face was damp with sweat.

"Time to go," he said.

SIXTEEN

They rode in silence, Hicks at the wheel, Crissa shotgun. Sandoval was behind her, looking out the window. All the weapons were disassembled and back in the tac bag, along with the balaclavas and jumpsuits.

A car passed them in the opposite direction, didn't slow. She flipped down the visor, watched Sandoval in the mirror there. If they planned to kill her, he'd be the one to do it. A shot to the back of the head, then her body dumped in the desert. The last witness to what happened back there, what they'd done.

He saw her watching him, leaned forward, touched her shoulder.

"Hey," he said. "I'm sorry. I got a little rattled back there, that's all. We all did."

She drew away from his hand. "Rattled? That what you call it?"

"Hey, he called the play. We told him to stop. He didn't. There wasn't much choice."

"We could have caught him," she said. "Brought him back."

"Maybe, maybe not. But we'd all be fucked if he made it into those hills, wouldn't we? We'd never find him. I did what I had to do."

"No one wanted it this way," Hicks said without turning. "But it happened. It's over."

Sandoval said, "She's not hearing you, man."

"You didn't have to do that," she said. "There was no reason."

She felt a tightness in her stomach, the first pulse of nausea. She couldn't be sick. Not here, not in front of them.

"You want us to drop you off?" Hicks said. "You can walk back, wait around for the highway patrol, tell them what happened. That what you want?"

The Cherokee's headlights cut through the darkness. On either side, an endless expanse of nothing.

"I know we're all emotional right now," Hicks said. "But we need to use our heads. We're still on our timetable."

Her cell phone began to buzz. They'd crossed into the service area of another tower. She took it from her jeans pocket, dropped it. Her hands were trembling. Hicks looked across at her.

The phone buzzed again on the floor. She picked it up. When she answered, Chance said, "We're on schedule. Transfer was a bitch, had to back the trucks tailgate to tailgate. But it's done. I'm en route. How'd things go on your end?"

She took a breath. "We'll talk later." Sandoval was watching her.

"You all right?" Chance said.

"I'm fine. Something unexpected came up."

"Anything I should know about right now? If so, you need to tell me."

"No. It doesn't affect you. Just stay on schedule. What about the others?"

"Soon as we did the transfer, they booked. Fine with me. That little guy made me nervous. I'll ask you again: Is there anything I need to know?"

"No."

"And you're okay?"

"I am." Knowing then they couldn't risk killing her until the truck got where it was going. If she fell out of contact with Chance, if he couldn't reach her, it would spook him. He'd ditch the truck, head off on his own.

"You don't sound it," he said.

"This phone's done. I'll call you in a little while from another one."

"Right," he said. "Later."

She ended the call, turned the phone over, and pried off the back cover. She tugged the SIM card free, snapped it in half, then powered down her window and tossed it out. The battery went next, the phone itself a mile after that.

"You should both do the same," she said.

"We will," Hicks said. "You okay?"

"Why wouldn't I be?" She looked out across the blackness of the desert. The moon hung low over the mountains.

"There really was no other way, you know," Hicks said. "We couldn't just leave them there after what happened. Four witnesses, only one way that was gonna play out. All of us in prison. Death row maybe."

"If we're caught, that's five felony murder counts," she said. "For all of us. Whether we pulled a trigger or not."

"Like I said, we didn't have a choice."

"Forget her, *jefe*," Sandoval said. He sounded almost cheerful. She could hear the release of tension in his voice. It was the way she usually felt herself after doing work, getting away. But not this time.

"Minute that dumb fuck took a runner, there was only one way it could go," Sandoval said. "She doesn't understand that. But give her time. She will."

She looked back at him. "You were so concerned about witnesses, why didn't you kill me, too?"

"I almost did." Sandoval grinned. "Heat of the moment and all that. Fuss you were making, it seemed like the right thing to do at the time. But your boyfriend here talked me out of it."

She looked at Hicks, wondering how much he'd told him. He kept his eyes forward. She wanted to be out of there, far away from the two of them. Realizing now how foolish she'd been. She'd thought she had a handle on everything, every detail, all of it under control. And then it had all come apart as she watched.

There was more traffic from the opposite direction. They passed through a small town that was gone as suddenly as it appeared. Beyond it, Hicks slowed, then turned down a side road that led to the abandoned ironworks he'd scouted two days before. Their headlights passed across the front of the massive building, reflected off the few panes of glass left in its windows. One smokestack still stood, but another had toppled into a side yard.

The transfer car was parked here, a rented Hyundai. Sandoval would take the Cherokee, wipe it down, ditch it. The tac bag with the guns would go into a flooded quarry they'd found two miles away.

Hicks parked the Cherokee behind a pile of rusted girders, killed the engine, but left the headlights on. They got out, and

Sandoval brushed past her, took a two-gallon plastic gas container from the back of the Cherokee. He got the jumpsuits and bala-clavas from the tac bag, dropped them into an empty lidless fifty-five-gallon drum. They would have hair on them, DNA. He poured gas over them, shook the plastic container until it was empty, then dropped it in. Fumes rose up.

"Stand back," he said. He took matches from his pocket, lit one and used it to touch off the others, then tossed the flaming pack into the drum. The gas-soaked clothes went up with a *whoomph* and a puff of black smoke.

"That's it for me, *jefe*. I need to get on the road, dump this shit. See you back at the house."

He opened the Cherokee's driver's side door, turned to Hicks, lifted his chin at her. "Tell her she's got nothing to worry about. *Se acabó.* Everybody gets to go home, right?"

She drove back to the house. They'd wiped it down that afternoon, destroyed everything that might tie them to the work. She'd al-ready stored her things in her rental, parked two blocks away. There was no reason for her to go into the house again. She wanted to get as far away as fast as possible.

"He's right, you know," Hicks said.

"About what?"

"About your thinking on all this later. Realizing it was the only way."

"Leave it."

He looked at his watch. "Still on time. We did pretty well as far as that goes. Hopefully your guy gets where he's supposed to be."

"He will."

He looked out at the dark desert.

"Used to be," he said, "when Sandy and I worked, we didn't have to worry about afterward. Generally we got away with whatever shit we did, didn't have to worry about the law. End of the day, only concern was whether our direct deposit went through on time that week."

She looked at him, then back at the road. The moon hung full and red, seeming to hover directly over the highway.

"You don't get it, do you?" she said. "It's not just about you. You put us all in the jackpot back there."

"One thing they teach you in the Corps is how to improvise. That's what we did."

"You didn't have to kill them."

"Spare me the sermon. And save that thief-with-a heart-of-gold bullshit for somebody else. You telling me you never pulled a trigger on anyone?"

"Only when I had to. When there was no way around it."

"Well, there was no way around it this time either. We wanted things to go one way, and they didn't. So we played the hand we were dealt. Big-boy rules."

"It was sloppy. A waste."

"Maybe so. But we did what we did. And now it's over."

They were passing by car dealerships, strip malls. The turnoff for the development was coming up. She signaled, changed lanes, eyes on the rearview, waiting for flashing lights to appear, for a Nevada highway patrol cruiser to come up fast behind them.

"I'll call the old man later," Hicks said. "Let him know what happened."

"He'll be thrilled."

"Well, it's a good news, bad news scenario, isn't it? And the good outweighs the bad. He got what he wanted, that's all that counts."

"All that counts with you, too?"

"That, and what he's paying me. You might feel differently, too, when the rest of those transfers go through for you and your people."

"No transfers this time," she said. "Cash."

"You don't trust him?"

"It's got nothing to do with that."

"I'll say one thing. It was good working with you. I was right, you're a pro."

"Drop it."

"We worked well together," he said. "Might be something worth exploring again."

"No chance."

He nodded, looked away. "That guy you told me about, Wayne? He ever getting out?"

"Why do you care?"

"Just saying. Time's short, you know. You have to make the best of what you got. And sometimes the best thing is right in front of you."

"I don't think so."

He grinned, looked out the window again. After a moment, he said, "Sandy would have shot you if I hadn't waved him off. You realize that, right? He genuinely does not give a shit. I saw him take out a whole house full of *hajjis* once, with just a couple of frags and an M-16. Women, children, he didn't give a fuck."

"That supposed to scare me?"

"No, I'm just saying. Extreme circumstances require extreme responses, you know?"

"Just leave it."

"I need to know you're okay with this."

She looked at him.

"We're all in the same situation," he said. "Your people, too. Like you said, felony murder, regardless of who pulled the trigger. You say anything to anybody, you're putting yourself in it, too."

"That what you're worried about?"

"A little."

"Don't."

"I need to know you're okay with it. And I need to hear you say it."

"That a threat?"

He didn't answer.

"And what if I told you to go fuck yourself?" she said.

He grinned. "Then I'd take that as a yes."

She shook her head slowly, angry at herself for what had happened, for not being able to stop it when things went bad. For being there in the first place.

They were almost at the house. She'd leave before Sandoval got back. No advantage to sticking around here, only risk. She'd drive south into Arizona, drop off the rental in Kingman, then go to the Amtrak station and catch the first train headed east. Leave the desert and all its blood behind.

SEVENTEEN

Halfway across Arizona, she texted Chance the number of the TracFone she'd bought in Kingman. It was always safer to travel by train after a job went bad. Easier to stay under the radar, not leave a paper trail.

It was after midnight, unbroken darkness outside the window. She'd been slipping in and out of sleep, the tension of the day still on her. The first time she woke, she was unsure where she was. Then the memory of what had happened came flooding back.

Her phone buzzed. "Where are you?" Chance said.

"Headed home."

"I heard there was trouble."

She straightened in the seat. "Where did you hear that?"

"CNN. What happened?"

She wondered how long it had taken them to find the dead men, how much they'd pieced together so far.

"It got out of hand," she said.

"You couldn't stop it?"

She took a breath, let it out slow. "No."

"What now?"

"Nothing changes. I'm making arrangements for payment. Cash this time."

"Good."

"Where are you?"

"Airport, waiting on my flight."

"How'd the drop-off go?"

"Just like you said. I pulled up outside the port, didn't even have to go through the gate. Last mile or so, there was a car following, three guys inside. Made me nervous at first. But I parked it, left the keys in the ignition, wiped everything down, got out, walked away. Nobody followed me. Caught a cab. Got here with no problem."

"What about the others?"

"Far as I know, they're already on a plane somewhere. I'll feel better when I'm on one, too. This shit's going to blow sky-high."

"I know."

"This complicate the money issue?"

"I'll make sure it doesn't," she said.

"After all that happened, last thing we need is trouble on that end."

"I'll take care of it."

"You need to look out for yourself, too. Let me know what you hear."

"I will." She ended the call, looked out at the night.

* * *

When Hicks came out on the balcony, Cota was leaning with both hands on his cane, looking off into the distance.

Without turning, he said, "Am I making a mistake, letting you back here?"

"No," Hicks said. "You're not."

Cota turned toward him. "Convince me."

"What do you want me to tell you, Emile? It's done. That's the important part."

He put his hands in the small of his back and stretched. He'd caught a late flight from McCarran to LAX, taken a cab here. Sandoval had come on a separate flight, was staying at a hotel on the strip.

"I spent most of this evening talking to various law enforcement agencies," Cota said. "In particular, the Nevada state police and the FBI. There'll be quite a bit more of that tomorrow, I imagine."

"You knew that would happen."

"I did," Cota said. "But I thought we would be discussing a truck hijacking or a robbery. Not a mass murder."

Hicks looked over the balcony at the flagstones below, the floodlit fountain, closed his eyes and smelled the jasmine.

"Well?" Cota said.

"Your stuff got where it was supposed to go, Emile, right? On time and as promised?"

"It did. I heard from the buyer a little while ago. It's already at sea."

"Then it's not your problem anymore. That's something worth celebrating, isn't it? I need a drink. You?"

He went back into the room, to the side bar near the big table.

The ceiling fans turned slowly. He poured scotch into two square glasses, heard Cota limp in behind him.

"No problems with Customs?" Hicks said. He leaned against the table.

"Not that I'm aware of."

Hicks handed him a glass. "How does that work, exactly? Getting something that big out of the country, no one sounds an alarm?"

"Same method by which it got in," Cota said. "Money in the right hands. Enough to make them willing to look the other way when a victimless crime occurs. At least that's what it was supposed to be."

"Have a seat, Emile. You don't look well." He seemed older in the light, eyes pouched, face wet with perspiration.

Cota slumped into a chair, rested his cane on the table, set the glass next to it.

"You been taking your meds?" Hicks said.

Cota ignored him, lifted the glass, drank. His face was pale.

Hicks sipped his own drink. "You all right?"

Cota nodded. "It's warm in here. That's all."

Hicks drew up another chair, sat. "Let's keep things in perspective, Emile. You always knew it could go bad out there."

"I did. And I was prepared for that. What I wasn't prepared for was the enormity of the complications."

"You've got nothing to worry about."

"You sound sure of yourself."

"No one can be sure of everything. But you play the odds."

"I'm not a gambler," Cota said.

"Neither am I. Is Katya here? I didn't see her when I came in."

Cota shook his head, took a handkerchief from a shirt pocket and wiped his forehead. "She has the evening off. She'll be back tomorrow."

"Don't sweat the FBI. It's only natural they'd question you. Just remember, you're the victim here. It's your property that was stolen."

"I'll try to keep that in mind."

"They got nothing. They'll pressure you a little bit, see if they get a whiff of something bent, but outside of that, what are they going to do? You're covered all around."

"I'll need to pay that woman and her people as soon as possible, to keep them quiet."

"That's a good idea. They'll want cash this time, though."

"I anticipated that as well." He wiped his forehead again. "But, to be honest, I'm thinking that maybe you made a mistake."

"How's that?"

"Perhaps you should have left them out in the desert with the others, delivered the truck yourself."

Hicks shook his head. "A bunch of convicted felons lying dead by the side of the road? People with fingerprints on file, police records, known associates? That would have been a bad move."

"And there's your man to be concerned about."

"Sandy's back already. We'll put a transfer through tomorrow for the rest of his money, then we're square. You don't need to worry about him."

"And what do I need to worry about?"

"Way I look at it," Hicks said, "not much of anything. Sit tight, let all this blow over. You get the balance from your buyer, what you're owed?"

"He was as good as his word. The funds went through tonight, into the bank in Geneva, as promised. No issues with that aspect of it at least."

"Then it's done. You carve my three hundred K out of that yet?"

"Not yet, but I will."

"Then neither of us has anything to worry about. This time though, I think I'd prefer it in cash as well."

Cota looked at him.

"I did my part," Hicks said.

Cota raised his glass again, drank. "I'll move the necessary funds stateside. I won't keep you waiting."

A breeze shifted the curtains.

"I'm going to crash here tonight, I think," Hicks said. "It's been a long day."

"You feel the need to keep an eye on me in the aftermath of all this? Afraid I'll do something rash?"

"I didn't say that." He grinned, finished his scotch, stood, stretched again. "Don't look so glum, Emile. You pulled it off. You got what you wanted."

Cota looked up at him. "Did I?"

EIGHTEEN

The house was dark and silent. Crissa dropped the gear bag with her clothes in the foyer, tapped in the code to disable the alarm.

She'd taken Amtrak to Penn Station in Newark, then an NJ Transit train south to Bradley Beach, caught a taxi from the station. Nearly two days on the train, and only a few hours of sleep along the way.

She walked the empty rooms, looking for a sign someone had been there in her absence. The .32 Beretta Tomcat was still in its holster clipped beneath her bed. From force of habit, she took it out, ejected the magazine to make sure it was fully loaded, checked the round in the chamber. The gun seemed somehow uglier now, after what had happened, cold and alien in her grip. She slid the magazine back in, returned the gun to its holster.

There was a single bottle of Medoc left in the wine rack in the kitchen. She opened it, poured a glass, took it out on the deck along with her phone. The motion detector above the door clicked on, bathed the backyard with light.

Dusk now. Early October, but Indian summer still hanging on. To the east, out past the mouth of the inlet, she could see the running lights of fishing boats heading out for the night. To the west, traffic was sparse on the drawbridge that connected Avon and Belmar. On summer nights, the bridge was often an unbroken line of taillights. But the season was over now, the tourists few.

Steps led down to the sloping backyard and the small dock beyond. It had come with the house; she'd never owned a boat. Nearly all of the homes on the inlet had private docks, but the summer residents were mostly gone, had dry-docked their boats at marinas or had them crewed south to Florida or the islands. She knew none of her neighbors, and the houses on both sides of hers were usually empty by September.

She sat on the steps, sipped wine, set the glass beside her. She was overtired, her legs restless. She hoped there were some Lunesta left in the medicine cabinet. Knew she'd need one to sleep tonight.

She called the number she had for the limousine company in Kansas City, listened to the line buzz. When a woman answered, Crissa said, "I need to talk to Sladden."

"There's nobody here by that name."

"This is a new phone, so he won't recognize the number. But tell him it's Ms. Wynn. I'm home."

"I'm sure I can't help you."

"Right," Crissa said, and broke the connection. They followed the same routine each time.

She'd just finished the glass when the phone buzzed. An 816 area code—Kansas City—but a different number than the one she'd called. Sladden being careful.

"Ms. Wynn?"

"I'm home."

"I heard. Heard some other things, too. Our friends from the Northeast have been asking about you." Keegan and McBride.

"Tell them I'll have something for them soon."

"They're a little anxious, given recent events."

"I know. Give them this number if they want to talk to me. I'm working it out."

"They're concerned about the logistics this time. They don't think the prior arrangement will do."

"They've got nothing to worry about. I'll take care of it." Feeling the irritation now. "You told them that, right? That I was good for it?"

"I tried."

"I'm making arrangements. It'll take a couple days at most. Tell them that. Or they can call and I'll tell them myself."

"I'll pass that on."

"And I'll have something for you, too." The finder's fee she gave him bought his silence as much as his contacts.

"What I like to hear," he said.

"I'll be in touch this week, let you know the details." She ended the call.

There was no sense stalling. She punched in numbers. When Hicks answered, she said, "Are you with him?"

"You mean that literally or figuratively?"

"Don't screw around. Is he there?"

"He is."

"Put him on."

There was silence, the phone being handed over. Then Cota said, "Yes."

"Your guys messed up."

"I'm aware of that. It was regrettable."

"It was more than that. You owe me money."

"I'm aware of that as well. I've begun the process."

"No process. Cash this time. He should have told you."

"He did, but I was hoping I could convince you otherwise."

"You can't. And you're going to put in another fifty K on top of what you owe."

"A penalty fee?"

"Something like that." She'd divide the fifty between Chance and the others. It would help smooth feathers.

"I guess I have no right to complain," he said.

"You don't."

"Still, I'll need a day or two to get this together. Then there's the question of delivery. I'm guessing you're no longer on our part of the continent. So transporting such a sizable sum over long distances has intrinsic challenges and risks."

"Just get it ready," she said. "You'll hear from me." She hung up.

She sat there for a while, listening to the sounds of the night, the traffic on the bridge, the far-off clang of a buoy. In her mind, she heard other sounds. The snap of rifle bolts slamming home again and again. The low moan of a dying man.

But Hicks was right, she thought. It's done. And there's nothing you can do about it.

She picked up the glass, went back in, pulled the sliding glass door closed behind her. In the living room, she turned on the wall-unit radio to chase the silence away. It was tuned to WQXR, the classical station out of New York. Berlioz's *Symphonie fantastique* filled the room.

She'd take a hot shower, more than likely finish the bottle. Tomorrow she'd worry about what came next. For now, she was home.

The bar was on a corner lot in Charlestown, at the bottom of a sloping industrial block. No sign above the door. Across the street was a high fence, traffic moving on the freeway beyond and below.

She parked on a side street, locked the car. A four-hour drive up from New Jersey in her leased Ford Fusion. Almost nine P.M. and no one on the streets. Cooler up here. She wore her leather car coat, kept her hands in her pockets.

The exterior of the bar was brown shingles, neon beer signs in the windows. Inside it was dark and narrow, a long bar with green vinyl stools on one side, high-walled booths on the other. On the walls, an Irish flag, maps of the old country, coats of arms. There was an ATM near the bar, and an old-fashioned phone booth in the back, next to a curtained doorway. No TV, no jukebox. Half a dozen serious drinkers on the stools. The room smelled of stale beer, cigarette smoke, and floor polish.

A white-haired bartender was drawing a pint. He looked at her for a moment, then nodded at one of the booths.

Keegan sat facing the door. In front of him were an empty pint glass, a black plastic ashtray, and a pack of Newports atop a folded newspaper.

She slipped in across from him. "Funny. Couldn't find this place in the Michelin guide."

He blew out smoke, ashed his cigarette in the tray. "Fancy that."

The bartender came over, set a full pint down, said, "Miss?"

Better to have a drink in front of her while she was here. She nodded at the pint. "What's that?"

"Murphy's," the bartender said.

"That's fine." He took the empty, went off.

"You made it back," Keegan said. "Almost surprised, after that cock-up out there. Saw it on the evening news, I did."

"It could have gone better. But it's over now."

"Not quite."

"Reason I'm here." The smoke was making her eyes water. She squinted, looked at the drinkers at the bar. One of them was younger than the others, wore a motorcycle jacket and work boots, was watching them in the bar mirror. He had a pint in front of him but hadn't touched it since she'd come in.

She nodded toward him. "One of yours? If not, he seems a little too interested in what's going on over here."

"Don't worry about him."

She heard the front door open. A moment later, McBride slid in beside her. He wore a thigh-length black leather jacket, had a thin growth of beard now. She moved over to give him space. "Am I late?" he said.

She looked at him, feeling the first stirrings of danger. The bartender brought her pint, set it on a paper coaster with a shamrock on it, looked at McBride.

"Killian's," McBride said. "And a Tullamore, too."

When the bartender was gone, McBride said, "Had a look. She's alone."

"I could have told you that," she said.

She slid over a few inches, to put more space between them. She and McBride were the same height, so that would be an advantage. If she had to, she could drive her elbow into his throat, push him out of the booth, head for the door. Take her chances with Keegan and the other one if they came after her.

McBride reached for the pack of Newports, bumped against her. She felt the weight in his left-hand jacket pocket. He took Keegan's cigarette from the ashtray, used it to light his own. More confident now than he'd been out West. He was back in his own element, his world.

The bartender brought his pint and a shot glass of amber liquid. When he was back behind the bar, she took the thick envelope from her inside pocket, set it beside the ashtray. "Just so there are no misunderstandings."

Keegan didn't look at the envelope, said, "And what would that be?"

"Twenty thousand," she said. "Ten each. Call it a down payment on what you're owed."

She'd taken the money from her personal account, would replace it when she got the balance from Cota. She needed to keep these two on her side in the meantime, allay their fears.

"I'm sure I don't know what you're talking about," Keegan said. "But if I did, I might say ten isn't enough."

"Like I said, it's a down payment."

"We're on the installment plan, are we?"

"I'm expecting the rest soon. When I have it, I'll contact you, and we'll meet. Here again if you want."

Keegan drew on his cigarette. McBride moved closer to her until their elbows touched. She pulled hers back, looked at him.

"Sean," Keegan said. "Manners."

"We agreed on a hundred for each of you," she said. "I negotiated another ten per man. Which means even with this"—she touched the envelope—"you've still got fifty each coming."

"I would have been much happier," Keegan said. "If you'd brought it with you."

"I don't have it yet. But I will soon."

"Thing of it is," Keegan said. "How do I know, once you walk out that door, we'll ever see you again?"

"You'll have to trust me on that. Or at least more than you have so far."

"What's that mean?" Keegan said.

McBride reached past her to ash the cigarette. With her left hand, she caught his wrist, pinned it to the table. As he tried to pull back, she reached into his pocket with her other hand, felt metal, drew out the gun, a snub-nosed .38. She brushed the tail of his jacket back, pushed the muzzle into his side just above the belt.

McBride froze. She twisted the gun deeper into the soft flesh there, finger on the trigger, the movement hidden beneath the table, Keegan watching her.

"Trust," she said, "also means not coming heavy to a meeting when there's no reason to. It sets the wrong tone."

She took the gun away, felt McBride relax. She released his wrist, and he jerked his hand back. She set the gun atop the envelope. Keegan moved the newspaper to cover it.

"Think about it," she said. "If I planned to screw you on this, would I even be here?"

Keegan gave her a half-smile, said, "Point made." McBride's face was red.

"If our friend in Kansas City had any doubts about me," she

said, "he wouldn't have put us together. He vouched for both of you. I'm guessing he did the same for me."

"He did," Keegan said.

"Then you know we're all professionals here. So there's no reason to act otherwise."

McBride reached for the gun. Keegan slid it out of his reach, still hidden beneath the newspaper. McBride sat back.

The man at the bar had swiveled on his stool, was watching them. Keegan looked at him, shook his head. After a moment, he turned around again.

"You're getting more than you're due," she said. "Consider the envelope a bonus, for being patient."

"Patience is one thing," Keegan said. "But situations like this, that go bad that way, it's not exactly normal business, is it? It's what you'd call special circumstances. The kind of situation where people panic, start making deals."

"No one's making any deals."

"That you know of."

"I can speak for Chance as well. No one's making any deals."

"We want cash," McBride said.

She ignored him. Keegan drew on his cigarette, then stubbed it out in the tray. "How soon?"

"Couple days, maybe," she said. "I'm waiting to hear back, to set up a time and place. And yeah, cash this time. I've already seen to that. No deposits. No transfers."

"Good."

"It'll take a little planning to pick the right location, right time. I'll let you know as soon as it's done."

"You won't have to do that," Keegan said.

"Why not?"

"Because we'll be coming with you."

She shook her head. "Not a good idea."

"It wasn't a suggestion." The smile gone from his face. "You talk about trust. It's a two-way street, isn't it? You find out when the pickup is, you call me, we all go together. That way no one gets confused or concerned. Everyone's on the same page."

"Listen," she said. "I respect the work you two did out there, the way you handled your end. But it's better I see this through myself. I'm the one they've been dealing with. They won't like my bringing someone else along."

"Then you'll just have to explain things to them, won't you?"

She looked at him, thinking it through, knowing she had to offer them some reassurance, something beyond the cash she'd brought.

"All right," she said after a moment. "I'll tell them. See what they say."

"I'm sure you can be very persuasive," Keegan said. "And in this case, you'll have to be."

"Why's that?"

"As I said, this isn't a suggestion. Or a request."

She sat back. The man at the bar was watching them in the mirror again.

"I'll talk to them," she said. "That's all I can promise. Now I need to get back on the road. Long drive."

"Where to?"

She didn't answer, said to McBride, "Mind?"

Without looking at her, he slid from the booth, stood. She got out.

"One thing," she said to Keegan. "Don't have your boyo at the bar, or anybody else that might be outside, try to follow me. I'll spot them, and I'll lose them. And then we're back on less-than-friendly terms again."

He raised both hands, palms out, let them fall. "I wouldn't think of it."

"I'll be in touch," she said.

NINETEEN

A warm breeze blew in from the ocean, brought the smell of the sea. She sat at the wrought-iron table on her deck and sorted through the mail she'd picked up that morning. Junk mostly, an electric bill, an envelope from Rathka. She kept a box at the small brick post office downtown, under the name Linda Hendryx, the one she'd used to buy the house. She kept other post boxes in other towns, under different names.

She was still tired from the drive the night before, and she'd slept poorly, even after three glasses of wine. The image of the bound men facedown in the sand, blood on the stone behind them, wouldn't leave her.

Rathka had sent her a deposit statement. Cota's advance payment had been routed through her bank in St. Lucia. Eventually Rathka would layer it into the businesses she'd invested in, and part of it would make its way back to her in the form of a monthly interest check.

On the table, her cell began to vibrate. Hicks calling back. She'd phoned him earlier that day, gotten his voice mail, left her new number.

"Good news," he said.

"What's that?"

"I think we're all set."

There was a subtle shift in the light around her. Gray clouds were gathering over the ocean.

"The essential problem hasn't changed, though," he said. "It's a lot of risk driving that kind of cash around. With that extra fifty, we're talking three hundred K."

"There's always risk. I'm sure you can work it out."

"But I want to minimize it, too, if possible. Some cop pulls the car over, gets nosy and starts to search, next thing you know, his bumfuck department's buying armored personnel carriers with your money."

"Still your money at that point. It wouldn't cancel the debt."

"Why am I not surprised? Always a hard-ass when it comes to bargaining, aren't you? Right from the jump."

"No," she said. "I'm not. We made a deal, and we'll both stick to the terms. What's simpler than that?"

"Still, a good payday for a couple hours' work."

"A month's work. Not to mention the risk over how it played out. You're concerned with the amount? How much did he make on the deal?"

"What's that got to do with it?"

"That's my point. I'll pick a place for the handover. You be there with the money. Then we're done."

"That bag will get packed in L.A.," he said. "Let's say we leave it in a car trunk, maybe a rental, park it somewhere. You come out here, get the keys, check the goods, drive it away. Take the car wherever you're going, ditch it whenever you want."

"I'm not going out there."

"Then pick a place, maybe halfway between us. We'll split the distance—and the risk."

She'd thought about options on the drive back from Boston. She didn't want him to know what state she was in, which direction she'd be coming from, didn't want to meet anywhere too far east. Once she had the money, she'd cut all ties with him, cover her trail.

"Phoenix," she said. "Downtown."

"That's a hike. Four hundred miles from here at least. You're talking six, seven hours on the road."

"You'll manage. I'll pick the spot, tell you where to drop off the car. You driving?"

"Hell, no. That's what delegating's for. Sandy maybe."

"I don't like that idea."

"What am I supposed to do, hire some guy off the street to drive a car cross-country with three hundred grand in it? How do you think that'll work out?"

She gave that a moment, knew he was right. "Then he leaves the car where I say. Puts the keys somewhere I can find them, takes a walk. Catches a bus back, whatever. But there's nobody near the car. If there is, I go home, and you still owe me the three hundred."

"Pretty confident, aren't you?"

"Confidence has nothing to do with it. This is business. How soon can you have it?"

"I'll have to see. That's a lot of cash to get together. It'll need to be counted and packed. Maybe by this weekend we'll be able to . . ."

"Day after tomorrow," she said. "He brings the money, waits somewhere in town. I call you, tell you where he needs to go. You call him, he makes the drop-off."

"That's not much time."

"Time enough. Have it ready."

"I'll do my best," he said, and was gone.

Clouds were pushing in from the east, the temperature dropping. Gulls squawked above her, backpedaling in the wind.

She called Chance.

"Payment's coming," she said. "Doing the pickup in a couple days. I'll drop off your share on my way home."

"You need me to come with?"

"No, I already have an escort." She told him about Keegan and McBride.

"Careful with those two," he said. "Not sure if I trust them after all this. You should bring me along."

"They want their money. I can't blame them. You've done enough, I'll handle this. How's Lynette doing?"

"Happy to have me back, I guess. Hard to tell sometimes."

"More reason not to come."

"Call me when it goes down," he said. "Soon as you can. If you change your mind, shout. I'll be on the next plane to wherever it is you need me."

"Thanks. But it's under control."

"This is no time for pride."

"I'll call," she said, and hit END. Then she punched in Keegan's number.

* * *

"That the car?" McBride said.

They were parked on a side street, Crissa at the wheel of the rented Camry, McBride beside her, Keegan in back. A half block up was Second Street and the parking garage she'd chosen. From here they had a clear view of the entrance and exit ramps. A car had just pulled up to the attendant's booth, driven inside.

"No," she said, and lowered the binoculars. The car was a Dodge Stratus. She'd been told to expect a Chevy Impala.

"Just about time, though, isn't it?" McBride said.

She looked at her watch. Five minutes to four. "Almost." They'd been here more than an hour.

Keegan lit another cigarette, blew smoke out his half-open window. "Patience."

It was a four-level parking garage in downtown Phoenix, surrounded by office buildings, concrete and glass. On one side was a redbrick plaza with planters and park benches. During the week the streets would be crowded, the garage almost full. But this was Saturday and there was little traffic. From what she could tell through the binoculars, the garage was half empty.

She'd gotten to Phoenix the day before. After checking into a motel near the airport, she'd driven around downtown, looking for someplace public but not too busy, that could be surveilled from a distance. She'd chosen the parking garage, had called Hicks an hour ago to give him the address, then picked up Keegan and McBride from their own motel.

"I don't like this," McBride said. "Being out in the open where any bugger can see us."

He wore a dark windbreaker, half zipped, too heavy for the weather. Keegan had on a floral print shirt, tail untucked. She assumed both were armed, had managed to acquire guns once they got out here. She wore a T-shirt and jeans, hadn't bothered with a weapon. If anything looked wrong, she'd walk.

On the console, her phone began to buzz. She picked it up.

"You should be seeing him any second," Hicks said. "I just talked to him. I'm assuming you're someplace close by."

"We'll see him," she said.

"The money's in a duffel in the wheel well. The car's clean, plates and registration are good. All the docs are in the glove box. Drive it anywhere you want. You get pulled over with it, you'll be fine. If they ask to search, that's another thing."

"I'll handle it," she said.

McBride was watching her. Keegan flicked his cigarette butt into the street.

Here was the Chevy now, an older model, dark blue, with California plates. Sandoval at the wheel, wearing sunglasses.

"That's the bastard," Keegan said.

Sandoval stopped at the light just before the garage ramp, his blinker on. She raised the binoculars one-handed. There was no one else in the car.

"He's here," she said into the phone. When the light changed, Sandoval pulled the Impala onto the entrance ramp, got a ticket from the machine outside the attendant's booth. The gate rose, and he drove into the shadows.

"Go check it out," Hicks said. "Call me when you're satisfied. Then we say good-bye." He hung up.

Five minutes later, Sandoval came out the street door, looked around, went to the crosswalk where two others were waiting for the light to change. Then he crossed, headed up Second Street, away from where they were parked, walking casually, no hurry.

"We should grab him," McBride said. "See what he has to say."

She shook her head, watched him walk a half block to the taxi stand. He spoke to the driver of a yellow cab, then got in the back. She watched as they drove away.

McBride started to open his door. "Wait," she said.

"For what?" McBride said.

She tracked the binoculars across the front of the garage, the plaza, the buildings on both sides. No signs of anyone else watching.

Keegan leaned forward, put a hand on McBride's shoulder, said, "She's right. We wait, keep an eye out, see if there's anyone else around. There's no rush now, right?"

She lowered the binoculars. If it looked safe, they'd divide the money right in the garage. Keegan and McBride would load their share in the empty duffel McBride had folded beneath his jacket. She'd take the bag Hicks had left, transfer the money to another suitcase back at the motel. Then she'd drive to Tucson, turn in her car, and get a long-distance rental for the ride home. She'd stop in Kansas City to give Sladden his cut, then on to Ohio and Chance.

Ten minutes later, no one had come in or out of the garage. She raised the binoculars again, trained them on the glass booth. The attendant was reading a newspaper.

"Enough," McBride said.

"This time he's right," Keegan said. "Enough."

"Maybe we should just take the car with us," McBride said. "Do the split somewhere else."

"I don't know anything about that car," she said. "Where it's been, whether the plates are good or not. I'm not taking any chances. We get the money, divide it, and we're gone."

"Agreed," Keegan said. She looked at him in the rearview. If they braced her inside, tried to take all the money themselves, there was nothing she could do about it. But it was too public a spot to risk gunfire, and the garage would have cameras. And they would know that if they took the money—her share and Chance's, too—and left her alive, she or Chance would hunt them down eventually. The risk outweighed the reward. It would be safer, smarter, for them to take what they were owed, leave it at that.

"Let's go," she said, and got out of the car. She put on her sunglasses, shoved her phone into her pocket, and started for the crosswalk, not waiting for them. Heard car doors open and shut behind her.

The pedestrian light was green, so she crossed the street to the stairwell door. The attendant was still buried in his paper. He didn't look over when she went through the door and up the concrete stairs.

Third floor. Her footsteps echoed in the stairwell. Below, she heard the street door open again.

She pushed open the third-floor door. Maybe fifteen cars on this level. The Chevy was parked halfway down on the left, nose to the interior wall, empty spaces on both sides. It was dim and cool up here, the concrete spotted with pigeon droppings. No one else around.

Beside the door was a reinforced glass case with a fire hose. Above that, a security camera mounted near the ceiling. She brushed her hand along the top of the case, felt the keys there in the dust, picked them up. She started for the car, not looking up at the camera as she passed. The stairwell door opened behind her.

Two Chevy keys on a ring, an electronic fob. She pushed the button, heard the doors unlock. Her phone vibrated. She pulled it from her pocket.

"Well?" Hicks said.

"I'm at the car."

"Everything go like you wanted?"

"So far." Keegan and McBride had come up behind her.

"Then call me when you're clear," Hicks said. "Let me know you're happy."

"Right." She ended the call. Beside her, Keegan said, "Keys."

"I've got them," she said, and McBride moved up on her left. She felt the pressure in the small of her back, the gun he held. The way they stood, it would be hidden from the camera.

"Keys," Keegan said again. She held them out, and he took them.

"Is it worth it?" she said. She still had the phone in her hand.

"Way we look at it," Keegan said. "All the trouble you put us through, to and fro, here and there, all that risk, another twenty isn't quite enough, is it?"

McBride cocked the gun, the hammer snicking into place. He ground the barrel into her spine, payback for Charlestown. At this range, with the muzzle flat against her, the shot wouldn't be loud. When she went down they could catch her between them, muscle her into the car. To the camera, it would look as if she'd fallen, and they were helping her.

"I should shoot you where you stand," McBride said into her ear. "Just for being a right bitch." He twisted the gun harder, sent a flash of pain up her back.

Keegan walked around the car, looking through the windows.

"Trunk," she said. "Wheel well." There was nothing else to do now, except let them take the money, then try to find a way to get it back.

Keegan pressed the fob button that opened the trunk. The latch clicked, and the lid rose two inches. McBride took the folded duffel from inside his jacket, tossed it onto the Impala's roof, then caught her belt and pulled her away from the car, not trusting her.

Keegan crouched, looked through the gap in the trunk, then straightened. "Let's see what we've got here," he said, and raised the lid the rest of the way.

The trunk was empty. No spare tire, no duffel bag. When the lid reached the top of its arc, she saw for the first time the thin wire there, and she knew.

She threw an elbow into McBride's face, twisted away from him, running. He fired at her, the bullet passing over her head, chipping concrete from the wall.

She looked back, saw Keegan turning away fast from the trunk, McBride looking at him, confused, and then it was too late. She saw the flash, dove for the ground, and it wasn't there, and then she was falling, falling, falling.

Hicks tried her number again. It didn't ring this time, went directly to an automated message that said the subscriber was no longer on the network.

The phone clicked, another call coming through. Sandoval.

"Where are you?" Hicks said.

"About a block away. I took a cab, then doubled back to watch, just in case. You're right, they couldn't wait."

"They?"

"The two micks were with her. The three of them went in, nobody came out."

"You sure of that?"

"I'm standing right here."

"How's it look?"

"Like someone called in an airstrike. Whole floor's burning like a motherfucker. Nobody walked away from that one."

"Stick around, call me back," Hicks said. "Let me know what you see."

"Right."

Hicks came in from the balcony. Cota rose from his seat by the cold, dead fireplace, leaning on his cane with both hands.

Hicks tossed the phone onto the chair he'd been sitting in a few minutes earlier, looked at Cota, and said, "It's done."

TWENTY

Water running over her, warm, constant, hissing from above. The crackling of flames somewhere behind her. The air full of smoke.

She tried to roll onto her side, but there was weight across her back. She pushed it away. McBride.

She was at the base of a concrete wall. Twenty feet away, the Impala was burning. All the glass blown out, the trunk lid gone. Thick black smoke billowed up, flattened against the ceiling. The sprinkler system was spraying water, the concrete floor wet with it, but it was having no effect on the flames. There was no sign of Keegan.

She tried to stand, put a hand on the wall to steady herself. Coughing made her ribs hurt. On the other side of the Impala, three spaces away, another car was on fire.

On her feet now. She took a step, kicked something, looked down to see a bare and blackened arm, severed at the shoulder, wondered whose it was.

A muffled alarm was sounding somewhere, and she realized then she couldn't hear out of her left ear. Just an echoing silence there, pressure.

Dizzy, she leaned back against the wall, moved along it, trying to get away from the flames. There was an explosion behind her, the other car's gas tank going up. A wave of heat blew over her.

Ahead of her, through the smoke, was the stairwell door. She held her breath, lurched toward it, hit the panic bar. The door flew open, and momentum carried her through. She fell hard onto the concrete landing, the door slamming shut behind her.

She coughed, sucked in cool air. In her nostrils was the scent of scorched hair, cooked meat. She could hear sirens somewhere far off, wondered how long she'd been unconscious.

Get up, she thought. Move. Walk.

She gripped the metal railing, pulled herself to her feet, used it for support as she went down the stairs. There was pain in her left leg. It wanted to fold under her. The right side of her head was numb, and when she touched her hair there, her fingers came away with blood.

She limped down the stairs, holding on to the railing with her left hand. Shouting outside and below, more sirens. On the second-floor landing, she pulled open the fire door, went in. She didn't want to go all the way down, run into cops or firefighters coming up the stairs.

Heading toward the exit ramp, she stopped to lean against cars when she had to. At the bottom of the ramp, she stood behind a pillar, tried to catch her breath. The attendant's booth was empty, and Second Street was full of people, all of them looking up at the flames.

She scanned faces, looking for Sandoval, wondering if he'd come back to watch, or finish the job. A fire truck, lights flashing, came around the corner and pulled to the curb, men spilling out of it. Firefighters began moving people off the sidewalk, toward the opposite side of the street.

She went down the exit ramp then, out into the street and into the clot of people. A man said something to her she didn't hear. She pushed past him.

When she reached the other sidewalk, she looked back. Smoke poured from the third floor of the garage, flames licking up the outside wall to the roof, the concrete already black from the fire. A flare inside, the *whump* of another explosion, and the smoke thickened.

A woman next to her was pointing at the sky. Crissa looked up, saw something in the air, caught in the thermal updraft from the flames. It drifted lazily down, its edges glowing red, and the crowd parted for it. It landed, faintly smoking, on the sidewalk. A charred piece of cloth about a foot square. A floral print. Keegan's shirt.

She turned and went through the crowd, no one paying attention to her, everyone watching the fire. When she reached the car, she felt a wave of dizziness. She put a hand on the hood to keep from falling, bent and vomited into the gutter.

"You all right?"

She looked up, and there was a uniformed cop standing there. She nodded, leaned back against the fender.

"You don't look it," he said. "EMTs will be here in a minute. You need to go with them."

"Right," she said, and looked past him to where his cruiser was parked halfway on the sidewalk, rollers flashing. "I will."

More sirens, another fire truck. The watchers had been pushed back farther. The cop turned from her, spoke into the body mike on his shoulder. The first truck had a hose going, was pouring water into the third-floor opening. Dark smoke roiled up into the blue sky.

She'd lost the phone, but she still had her keys. She unlocked the car, slipped behind the wheel, had a coughing fit that left her dizzy again.

An ambulance came up fast behind her, siren and lights going. It turned the corner, pulled up at an angle to the fire truck. The cop trotted toward it.

She gripped the wheel until her hands stopped shaking. Her head was throbbing, pain replacing numbness. There was a rhythmic pounding in her left ear, in time with her pulse.

She turned the rearview toward herself. Dried blood on her face. Her hair was singed on the left side, and there was a lump on her right scalp that triggered a surge of pain when she touched it. But no fresh blood. She had turned to her right just as the Impala went up. McBride had been in front of her, had taken the brunt of the peripheral blast, but she must have been thrown back, hit her head against the wall, blacked out. Concussion maybe. Or worse, a fractured skull.

She started the engine. More police cars out there now, parked at angles. She needed to get out of there before they blocked off the street. Uniformed officers were standing around talking, looking up at the fire. They'd be canvassing for witnesses soon.

She had to get to a phone, call Chance. One of the cops turned and came back toward her, the same one from before. He was saying something she couldn't hear, motioning for her to roll down her window. She raised a hand as if to acknowledge him, cut the wheel into a tight U-turn, watched him in the rearview as she drove away.

In the motel room, she dialed Chance's cell from memory. When it went to voice mail, she said, "It's me. Call me soon as you can," and read off the number on the front of the phone.

Her clothes reeked of smoke and gasoline. She left them on the bathroom floor, turned on the shower. She could hear better from her left ear now, though the sound of the water was still muffled. When she climbed in, the hot water on her scalp made her gasp. She shut her eyes, kept her head under the spray, trying not to cry out. When she opened her eyes again, pink water was circling the drain.

You fucked up, she thought. Bad. You're lucky to be alive.

All of it settling in on her now, what had happened, how close it had been. She thought about Maddie, the last time she'd seen her, at the playground, laughing, running. How close she'd come to never seeing her again.

She was trembling now, chills running through her. She made the water hotter, but it had no effect. Finally, she sank down in the tub, arms around her knees, steam rising around her, and shook.

They sat in the big first-floor living room, watching cable news on the wall-mounted plasma TV. On the screen was a helicopter shot of the burning parking garage, smoke rising up. Titles at the bottom of the screen read POSSIBLE CAR BOMB EXPLOSION IN PHOENIX, ARIZ. CASUALTIES UNKNOWN.

"They'll say it's terrorism," Cota said. He had a full glass of scotch in his hand, no ice. "The government will be involved, Homeland Security. Convince me there wasn't a better way to do this. A more circumspect way."

"The car's untraceable," Hicks said. "You don't have to worry about that. And this was the best way. The money was the only bait that would bring her. She was too smart, too careful. And it had to be someplace public. She wouldn't have gone for anything else."

"A little too public."

"I'd hoped they'd take the car somewhere, maybe to where the other one was, too, before they popped the trunk. That way we'd have gotten all of them at once."

"Then you miscalculated."

"No. I knew there was a chance this would happen, but there was nothing I could do about it. You can't cover every contingency, no matter how hard you try."

"And still, the job is only half done."

"We'll find Chance some other way. I have some ideas."

"And the man in Kansas City?"

"Him, too," Hicks said.

"You seem confident."

"It'll take them days—maybe months—to figure out what happened in there. Could be with her bringing those other two along, we caught a break. When they ID them, the cops might chalk it up to some sort of splinter IRA bullshit, if we're lucky."

"And you're certain the woman was in there?"

"I was on the phone with her just before it happened. She was right there, keys in hand, about to open the trunk. They'll be picking up pieces of her for weeks."

Feeling the doubt, but not saying anything. He had underestimated her in the past. It wouldn't feel done until he knew for sure.

"So what will you do now, about the others?" Cota said.

"Give it a break, Emile. I told you. I'm on it." He stood. "I'm going to go up, get some air."

He went up to the third-floor balcony, watched the sun setting over the ocean. He gripped the marble railing, drew in air, breathed out. Steady, he thought. You just need to be calm, careful, see it all through.

Footsteps behind him, the clack of the cane.

"You're troubled," Cota said.

Hicks shook his head, didn't turn.

Cota came out to stand beside him. "Is it the woman?"

Hicks looked at him. "Did I say that?"

"You don't have to. But I assure you, Randall, when you look back on this six months, or a year, from now, on all that we've done, all that we've had to do, you'll understand. Things happened just as they were supposed to. As they were destined to, even. It will all make sense then. We've done the right thing, all around. The best thing."

"Did I say different?"

"My main concern now is about the other one, Chance. What will his reaction be? These people sometimes have loyalties, don't they?"

"Only to money," Hicks said. "But we'll deal with him, one way or another."

"We have to wind down this thing we created, tie off the loose ends. Until then, it's not finished."

"I'll take care of it."

"You've got a plan?"

"Always."

"I didn't mean to question your efficiency."

"Then don't."

Cota looked off into the twilight, breathed deep.

"I appreciate what you've done for me, Randall," he said. "I do. The sacrifices you've made. The risks you took. I don't carry that lightly."

"Good. Because these other things, tying up these loose ends, it's going to cost you."

"I never thought otherwise. Still, in the long run, worth it all, don't you think?"

"For you, maybe."

"For both of us, Randall. You've more than earned your share of what's coming from the fruits of this transaction."

"Soon, I hope."

Cota patted his shoulder, said, "Soon enough," and went back inside.

Hicks got out his cell, called Sandoval.

"Yeah, *jefe*."

"Where are you?"

"Just left LAX. Got a car, heading your way."

"You see the news?"

"Saw some of it in the airport, waiting for my flight. That was beautiful, man, way you set it up. It do the job?"

"The first part. There's more work coming up."

"Say the word. I'm your man."

"It could be a little more complicated now. The people we're looking for, they'll know we're coming."

"Whatever. We'll get it done."

"Those guys of yours you told me about," Hicks said. "They still available?"

"If it pays right, yeah. Always."

"Call them," Hicks said.

TWENTY-ONE

When Crissa opened the door, Chance winced. "Jesus, you look like hell."

"Thanks. Come on in." She locked the door behind him.

He was carrying a Nike shoebox under one arm, set it on the bed. "What you wanted."

They were in a motel outside Cincinnati. She'd changed rental cars, spent thirty hours on the road, stopping only to eat and catch a couple hours' sleep parked in a truck stop rest area. She'd gotten in at midnight the night before, slept eleven hours before calling Chance. Her head still throbbed, but most of her hearing had returned.

"Any problems?" she said.

"No, it's clean. Right from the factory. There's a box of rounds in there, too. Tell me what happened."

She opened the shoebox. Inside was a bundle of tissue paper.

Beneath it, a Glock 40 with checkered plastic grips, smelling of gun oil. She took it out, ejected the magazine, checked it was full, then worked the slide to make sure the chamber was clear. The action was smooth, easy.

"Thanks," she said. She reseated the magazine, put the gun on the nightstand.

"You're burnt," he said.

She touched the left side of her face, where the hair had been singed. The skin there still stung. "It's nothing."

"Maybe you should sit down."

She sat on the bed. He pulled the room's single chair over. "It hurt?"

"Not too much anymore."

"Maybe you need to see a doctor."

She shook her head. "You talk to Sladden?"

"Talked to the woman who runs interference for him. Asked him to call me. He hasn't yet."

"He needs to know what happened."

"If he doesn't already. For all I know, he took off when he heard about that business in Nevada. He's smart. He knows when to pull his head back into the shell."

"Let's hope."

"Fill in the details. How did it play out?"

"C-4, I'd guess. Rigged to the trunk somehow."

"Hicks," he said. "That's his style. Question is, do they know you're alive."

"If they don't, they will soon. It'll buy me a little time, but not much."

"Time for what?"

"To figure out what I'm going to do next."

"What's there to do?" he said. "Christ, you were lucky to walk away as it is. It's done."

"They owe me money. You, too."

"I'll take the loss. Way things went, I want to stay as far away from the fallout as possible. You should, too."

"They might not let us."

"What's that mean?"

"That old man is trying to cover his tracks. Maybe he's panicking, trying to hedge his bets. Get rid of anyone might be a problem."

"You think they planned it that way? What happened in the desert? Killing those men?"

"I don't think so. But I don't know for sure."

"They might come looking for us, finish it up, is that what you're saying?"

"Maybe. I'm sorry for bringing you into all this."

"No way you could have known."

"Not good enough. Five people died out there. That shouldn't have happened. I let it get away from me. I fucked up."

"You didn't pull the trigger."

"Might as well have. It was my responsibility. I put it together."

"Nothing you can do about it now."

She got up, went to the window, pushed the curtain aside and looked out. The floodlit motel lot, then the interstate going past, nothing but fields on the other side. Knowing he was right. And knowing it didn't matter.

"You need to take some time," he said. "Think about this. You make a move, do it for the right reasons. I'll back you, whatever happens. You know that. But think it through first."

"Sladden was the only one knew all of us," she said. "And now you say he might be in the wind. Would he sell us out, if there was enough money involved?"

"Unlikely. He knows if he did, he'd never get the chance to spend it."

"Maybe I should make a trip to Kansas City. See what's what."

"And why would you do that?"

"If he's there, maybe I can straighten things out with him. Try to repair some of the damage I caused."

"I don't think he'd like that. Not with all this heat."

"I owe him some money, too. That he'll like. But mostly, I need to know where he stands. If Hicks or Cota contacts him again, I want to know about it."

He shook his head slowly. "It went bad. Nature of the beast. We all knew the risks. Keegan and McBride, too. Lay low for a while. I'll reach out to Sladden again when he surfaces, see what he has to say."

"If you can find him. How long a drive to Kansas City from here?"

"Eight, nine hours, maybe. But if you're going, I should go with you."

"No," she said. "This is on me. Go home to Lynette. I'll call you, let you know what I find out, how it went."

"You shouldn't go at all."

"I screwed up some things," she said. "I need to fix them."

Sandoval said, "Come on in, *jefe*. Grab yourself a beer. Every-body's here."

The hotel was in Chicago. When Hicks walked into the suite,

there were three men sitting around a table, drinking beer. He'd never seen them before, but knew their kind. Close-cropped hair, tight black T-shirts, tattoos. One had a long pink scar on the side of his neck.

Hicks nodded at them. He was tired from the flight, hadn't been able to sleep on the plane. Sandoval went into the kitchenette, came out with an open bottle of Dos Equis, handed it to him.

"Let me do the introductions," Sandoval said. He nodded at the man with the scar. "This is Banks. We used to call him Cicatriz back in 'Dad. For obvious reasons."

Banks nodded at him.

"And this ugly motherfucker's Finley." He was the youngest, dark hair, good-looking, wore a silver cross outside his T-shirt.

"And Schumann here, he's my partner. My *life* partner."

"You wish, *maricón*," Schumann said. He was blond, arms thick with muscle. His upper left arm was circled by a tattoo of a bandolier of .50-cal ammunition.

"Have a seat, man," Sandoval said. Hicks took the fourth chair. Sandoval sat on the arm of a couch. "You got some news for us?"

"I do," Hicks said, the three men watching him. "Deposits went into all your accounts today. Twenty K each. Another twenty when we're done."

"Sandy didn't tell us much," Schumann said. "Might help if we know some more. Like what exactly it is you're expecting from us."

"The mission's simple," Hicks said. "But there's two parts to it, maybe three, in different locations. I'll be along for most of it."

"Heavy work?" Finley said.

"Nothing you haven't done before."

"Speaking for myself," Schumann said. "That could mean a lot of fucking things."

"You've done more for less, I guarantee you," Sandoval said. "Everybody's gettin' paid. That's the important part."

"What about gear?" Finley said.

"I'll have everything you need," Hicks said. "Transport, too. You don't need to worry about any of that. I'll have you covered."

"Forty K's a lot of money," Banks said. "I figure we're going to have to earn it."

"You will," Hicks said.

Sandoval leaned forward between them, raised his bottle. They all did the same, clinked bottlenecks. Hicks touched his to the others' last.

"*Vive la mort,*" Sandoval said, "*vive la guerre . . .*"

"Fuck that *mort* bullshit," Schumann said. "We all work, and we all go home."

"That's right," Hicks said.

TWENTY-TWO

Sladden's limousine company was on Interstate 64 just outside the city. She didn't know his home address. They'd met only once, a year earlier, when she'd delivered his finder's fee for the work she'd done in Detroit. In his sixties now, he'd been a pro himself, back in the day, but his last prison bid ten years ago had broken him. Now he stayed on the sidelines, helping put together crews, acting as a go-between, taking his cut. It was safer, more lucrative.

She slowed as she drove by. The office was a small house with a parking lot in front instead of a lawn. Three Town Cars were parked on an adjoining lot, gleaming under lights. The office windows were dark.

She'd called the office an hour ago, but no one had answered, and no voice mail had picked up. Gone to ground, she thought, when he'd heard about Nevada.

She made a U-turn, headed back, then pulled into the lot of a darkened ice cream shop across from the office, killed the lights and engine.

Her watch said nine P.M. She took out the burner she'd bought that afternoon, tried Sladden's number again. It buzzed a dozen times. She hit END, called Chance.

"I'm here," she said. "Just drove by the office. Might be someone in there, I don't know. Tried his number again. No answer."

"Something spooked him."

On one side of the house, a driveway led around to a rear yard bordered by trees. From this angle, she could see a dark Lincoln parked there. It hadn't been visible from the highway.

"There's a car," she said. "But I don't see anyone moving around inside the house. And all the lights are off, far as I can tell."

"What are you going to do?"

"Not sure. Go take a look, I think. Maybe something in there tells me where he's gone. Might find a home address, too, be my next stop."

"Drive away."

"I can't. I need to know what the situation is. I don't want to be looking over my shoulder all the time, wondering if he turned, what he's thinking."

"He'd never rat. Never has, and he's had plenty of opportunities. And anyway, suppose he did already. How do you know there aren't half a dozen federal agents inside there with vests and shotguns, waiting for you to come through that door?"

"I don't."

"My point."

A car passed, its headlights briefly illuminating the front of the office, the parked limos.

"I should have come with you," he said.

"No reason to. I just need to talk to him if he's around here, see where he stands. And if he's in the wind, I need to know that, too, plan accordingly."

"Wait for me. I can be there by morning."

"No. Sit tight. I'll call you when I know something."

She shut off the phone, pulled on a pair of leather gloves. Still no sign of movement across the street. She got out, closed the door just short of latching, went around and opened the trunk. The Glock was in a paper bag under the spare tire in the wheel well. She eased the slide back to check the chambered round, then wedged the gun into her belt in the small of her back.

She zipped up her windbreaker, closed the trunk, waited. Two cars passed. When the highway was clear, she crossed quickly. The limo area would likely have video cameras, so she kept clear of it, went up the driveway. The Lincoln was parked by a side door, nose first against the house. She laid a gloved hand on the hood. It was cold.

A security light went on above the door, lit up the car. She stepped back out of its glare.

There were blue and yellow recycling buckets against the house. She took the blue one, upturned it, and slid it toward the side door, then backed into the shadows again, waited. After a few minutes, the security light clicked off again.

She could hear her own breathing, feel the beat of her heart. Five minutes by her watch, the night still, and then she took the Glock from her belt, moved up to the side door. The light went on again, and she stepped up onto the bucket, shattered the bulb with the gun butt. The yard fell dark again.

She got down, put the bucket back, then stood against the wall in the new darkness, waiting to see if the noise would draw anyone.

Another five minutes. She took out her penlight, switched it on, played the beam across the side door. Saw for the first time the black gap along the jamb. The door was closed but hadn't latched. She switched off the light.

She could walk away now, as Chance had said. Get back in the car, head home. But then she'd never know what she'd left behind here, or who might be coming after her.

The Glock at her side, she went up the three steps to the door, pushed it open with gloved fingers. Darkness inside, an acrid smell. She listened, heard nothing, then went in, switched on the penlight again.

Ahead of her, a dark empty kitchen. To the left, a narrow corridor with cheap paneling. Two doors opened off the hallway. She moved toward the first one, shone the light inside. A small bathroom, just toilet and sink. The second door was closed.

The hallway ended in a carpeted office. Two desks on opposite sides of the room, filing cabinets against the wall. The smell stronger here, bitter, scorched. Faint light came through the front windows.

Above one of the desks was an open metal cabinet, car keys hanging inside. Across the room, a small red glow. She raised the penlight, saw a credenza along the wall, a coffeemaker atop it, the red light at its base. That was where the smell was coming from. No coffee left in the beaker, just a burned crust along the bottom. A thin crack ran down the glass. She touched the switch, shut it off.

A car went by on the highway, its headlights coming through

the drawn shades, moving across the room. She waited until it passed.

Another smell in here, one she couldn't identify. She shone the penlight around. Next to the coffeemaker, a fax machine, color brochures lined up neatly on a table beside it. A copy machine in one corner. Beside it, a silver Mesa safe, the door open. There were papers strewn on the carpet around it, ledger books. She edged around the desk, bent to pick up one of the ledgers, and saw the body there.

It was a woman in her sixties, splayed out on the floor beside an overturned swivel chair. She wore a dress, had one nyloned leg tucked beneath her. Her eyes were open. There was a thick pool of blood under her head, dark spatter on the paneling behind.

All the desk drawers had been pulled out and emptied onto the floor—papers, brochures, office supplies. She imagined the way it must have happened. They'd come in the side door, moving fast. The woman at the desk here, standing when she saw them, then taking a round to the forehead. The blood on the floor was dark but still shone. She hadn't been dead long.

She played the light across the desks. Printers, but no computers, just cables leading nowhere. That meant they'd likely had laptops, and whoever had done this had taken them.

She went back down the hallway to the closed door. It was unlocked. She opened it, shone the penlight down wooden steps to a carpeted floor. She listened for a moment, then touched the wall switch inside the door. Fluorescent ceiling lights blinked on downstairs.

She switched off the penlight, put it away. Not wanting to go down there, but knowing she had to. The Glock in a two-handed grip, she moved down the steps quietly, gun up, waiting for a target.

There was a water heater against one wall, stacked boxes against another. More filing cabinets. And there in the center of the room, a man on his knees, shirtless, a dark hood over his head. His arms were extended above him, clothesline tied around his wrists, then to pipes that ran along the ceiling. He'd slumped forward, but the clothesline kept him from falling all the way. His chest and stomach were smeared with dark blood, crisscrossed with puncture marks, too small for bullets. The carpet below him was dark and discolored. The coppery smell of blood was thick in the air.

She let out her breath, lowered the gun, went to him. With one hand, she lifted the hood, knowing what she'd find.

Sladden's eyes were half open, his chin against his chest. There were about a dozen puncture marks on his chest, stomach, and sides, and there, at the base of his skull, what would have been the final one. When they were done with him, they'd ended it that way. But it had been a long death, and a slow one, and no way to know what he'd said while it was happening, what they'd asked him, how much he'd told them.

She dropped the hood on the floor, put away the Glock and took out her penknife. She couldn't leave him like this. Taking hold of one side of the clothesline, she used the short triangular blade to slice through it, then did the other. He fell forward stiffly, then onto his side.

There was nothing else to do here. She'd been too late again. She closed the knife, pocketed it, then went back up the stairs, shut off the basement lights, closed the door.

Back in the car, she called Chance, told him what she'd found.

She heard him inhale. Silence on the line, and then, "What do you think he told them?"

"I don't know, but it looks like they had him down there for a good long time. The office safe was open, too, and all the computers were gone. No telling what he kept on those. How much did he know about you?"

"A lot. We go back a long ways."

"Your address? Where you are now?"

"Yeah," he said.

"Not good."

"How about you?"

"Not much, I don't think. Everything we did was on burners or in person. Might be a good time for you and Lynette to take a trip, though."

"She's already gone. I sent her to her sister's in Iowa today. The more I thought about how things were playing out, the less I liked it. I told her it was temporary. She wasn't happy, but she went."

"Go with her. Stay out of Ohio for a while."

"Hell with that. I'm not going anywhere. Do you know how long it's been since I've had a real home, a place to call my own?"

"Better to leave. Think about it."

"I don't need to. This is my home. I'm staying."

"If they got your address from Sladden, they'll be on their way," she said. "Hicks and Sandoval, maybe others. We don't know how much of a head start they got."

"Fuck 'em," he said. "Let 'em come."

* * *

Hicks washed his hands in the filling-station sink, rubbed at the dried blood on the inside of his left wrist. The latex gloves he'd worn hadn't come up high enough. He palmed water in his face, looked at himself in the mirror. His eyes were sunken, bloodshot.

A knock at the restroom door. Sandoval said, "You okay, *jefe*?"

He tore brown paper towels from the dispenser, dried his hands. "What? You want to come in and hold it for me?"

"Just asking, man," Sandoval said. "You've been in there awhile."

He crumpled the wet towels, dropped them in the trash bin, went out.

"Just wanted to make sure everything was okay," Sandoval said. "You look pretty beat."

"I'm fine."

"It's been a long day. Lots of miles."

"It has."

The other three were standing around the rented Suburban, Banks pumping gas in the harsh glare of the island lights. Traffic flew by on the interstate beyond.

"Not for nothing," Sandoval said. "But a couple of the guys, they're wondering why you're not coming with us now."

"What did you tell them?"

"That it was none of their business. And they're not getting paid to ask questions."

"Right answer."

"We come all this way, though, I can understand. They're looking for you to call the shots with this next thing, right?"

"It's one guy. There's four of you. I'm sure you can handle it."

"I think you freaked them out a little, too. I mean, that was some off-the-chain Gitmo-level shit back there."

212 | Wallace Stroby

Hicks looked at him. "Got what we wanted, didn't we? I did what I had to do."

"Hey, I know. I'm just saying."

"Then tell them they need to man up. I have something else to take care of, needs to happen at the same time. That's why I'm not coming. You drop me at the airport. I'll be in touch after I land."

"What about those computers?"

"Ditch them somewhere. I got what I needed."

"This guy we're looking for. He might not even be there, right? He might be long gone."

"That's what you're gonna find out."

"If he ain't there, then what?"

"Then we'll see."

Banks finished with the gas, fit the nozzle back in the pump, looked over at them.

"How much they know about what happened back there?" Hicks said. "In Nevada?"

"Nothing. They didn't ask, and I didn't volunteer. They're here to do a job, *jefe*. They don't need to know the backstory. And you don't need to get any ideas."

"Good. Let's keep it that way."

They walked back to the Suburban. The others were already inside, Banks at the wheel, engine running. Sandoval got in the back. Hicks climbed into the front passenger seat. Banks looked at him.

"What are you waiting for, soldier?" Hicks said. "Let's roll."

TWENTY-THREE

Crissa stood at the kitchen window, looked up the gravel road to the wooden gates, everything falling into shadow as the sun went down.

"What is it?" Chance said behind her. He was sitting at the table, oiling a disassembled Ithaca pump shotgun, the parts laid out on newspaper. A lit cigarette hung from his mouth.

"I was wondering," she said. "If there's a way to block that road."

"There's some fifty-five-gallon barrels out back. Empty. I could load them in the pickup, put 'em out there, maybe string some barbed wire between them. Stop anyone trying to come down that hill in the dark."

She'd arrived late the night before, slept fitfully on the couch. Whenever she began to drift off, she saw the puncture wounds crisscrossing Sladden's skin, the final, fatal one at the base of his skull.

She moved to the side window, next to the door. Chance's pickup was in the driveway about ten feet away. Her own rental was parked out of sight in the barn. She looked across the cultivated field to the treeline, already darkening.

"You talk to Lynette?" she said.

"If you can call it that." He was fitting the shotgun parts back together. "Mainly I talked, and she pretended to listen. Not sure where we left it."

"It's good she's away from here. You should be with her."

"We went over that already." He opened a box of 12-gauge shells, began to feed them into the shotgun's receiver.

"What's on the other side of those woods?" she said. "Past the soy field."

"More woods."

"Fire roads?"

"Not around here." He worked the pump to chamber a shell, slid another into the receiver to replace it, then engaged the safety. "To the west, there's a good half mile of woods, then an old quarry. Only ways in and out of here, in a vehicle at least, are what I showed you, front gate and the road in back. Otherwise you're on foot." He set the shotgun on the table.

She took the Glock from her belt, eased back the slide to check the round in the chamber again, a nervous habit. She set it beside the shotgun. "What else have we got?"

"Thirty-eight Smith," he said. "The snub you saw. Up there." He nodded at the refrigerator.

She took the gun down. Rubber grips, two-inch barrel. Useless at anything more than fifteen feet, but a manstopper up close. She swung open the cylinder, saw all six chambers were loaded.

"More shells in the cabinet there," he said. "For both."

The Devil's Share | 215

She snapped the cylinder shut, put the gun back where it had been.

"He might not be coming," Chance said. "Could be Sladden didn't tell him anything."

She hit a wall switch. A floodlight went on outside the side door, illuminated the pickup. "Maybe. But we have to assume he did."

"This waiting," he said. "Makes me think about that other time. In the snow."

"Yes," she said. "Me, too."

"How long?" he said.

She looked at him. "What?"

"How long do you think they worked on him before they finished it?"

"I don't know. Long enough."

He shook his head. "Hell of a thing. He was an OG, I know. He played the Game. But still, to go that way . . . He didn't deserve it."

"Who does?" she said.

He cooked hamburgers for dinner, but she couldn't eat. There was a growing knot in the pit of her stomach. She paced the darkened house, checked the locks on the heavy front door. There was a chill in the air, so he'd built a fire in the living room fireplace. As it grew, the flames threw shadows against the walls.

She sat in an overstuffed chair, the Glock on a table beside her, looked into the flames. He turned off the kitchen light, came in after her. Somewhere in the house, a clock chimed nine.

"Beer?" he said. "No wine in the house, unfortunately. Neither of us drinks it."

She shook her head, growing drowsy with the darkness, the warmth of the fire on her legs. Her whole body seemed to ache; the past weeks, the driving, the lack of sleep, all of it catching up with her.

He put another split log on the fire. A dog barked far off somewhere.

She closed her eyes, began to drift, then snapped back awake. Chance sat on the couch, looking into the fire, his arms crossed. Wondering if it was all worth it, she thought. Endangering everything he had, running risks that might never be resolved.

"Any water out there?" she said. She needed to stretch her legs, clear her head.

"Refrigerator."

She got up and went into the darkened kitchen. The dog was still barking. She opened the refrigerator, light spilling out on the linoleum floor. There were half a dozen cans of Budweiser in there, some water bottles on the door shelf. She took one, cracked the cap.

He came up behind her, said, "I'll have one of those beers, I think," and a red beam of light centered on his chest.

"What the . . . ," he said, and she was already moving, dropping the bottle, ducking low, barreling into him. They hit a kitchen chair, went over and onto the floor. The front kitchen window dissolved in a cascade of glass, and something struck the wall over the counter.

She rolled off him. The red light tracked across the kitchen, looking for a target. A second beam came through the side window by the door, held steady. So there were at least two of them out there, with silenced weapons. Hicks or Sandoval, or both.

"Son of a bitch," Chance said.

The Glock was still in the other room. She crawled to the table, reached up and felt the stock of the shotgun, drew it toward the edge. Chance had pulled himself up, was sitting with his back to the wall, next to the interior doorway. The wandering laser passed along the walls again at head height, moving slow. The other beam stayed where it was.

"Do you think that . . . ," Chance said, and then the curtain over the shattered window puffed, and a round punched into the side of the refrigerator. Another ricocheted off the sink. He grunted. A third round cut a furrow across the tabletop. She pulled her hand back, then kicked a table leg hard. The shotgun fell off the edge and into her arms.

Without a target, whoever was outside was hoping to keep them pinned down. They would try to flank them next, she knew, send someone in the front or side door.

She looked at Chance. He was holding his left thigh. There was blood there.

He looked at her, and she thumbed off the safety, cocked her head toward the broken window. He nodded.

The curtain moved again, but just a breeze this time. She crawled across the linoleum, felt broken glass under her, flattened against the wall beneath the front window. The laser tracked across the room again, and a round hit the wall above Chance's head. He ducked. Plaster dust drifted down.

They'd come in closer now, up to the windows if they could, shoot any clear targets in the room. Then they'd come in hard through the doors, sweep through the house.

The sound of footsteps outside the window. She tried to remember if Chance had worked the pump after he loaded the shotgun, if there was a shell in the chamber. The laser cut through the air inches above her head, a different angle, the shooter closer.

She drew in breath, held it. Get moving, she thought. If you don't, you're going to die here, just like this. Do it. Move.

She raised up fast, pointed the shotgun through the broken window, and there was a figure there in the darkness, five feet away, using a tree as cover. She fired, the butt kicking back against her. In the muzzle flash, she caught a glimpse of a face she didn't know. The figure dropped away, the laser angling crazily upward, and she pumped and fired again, blew bark off the tree.

She sank back down, worked the pump to eject the smoking shell. Chance had taken the sportsman's plug out of the magazine, so the shotgun would hold six shells when fully loaded, five in the tube and one in the chamber. That meant she had four left until she could reach the table.

Footsteps on the gravel driveway. She didn't know if she'd hit anyone, but they'd be more cautious now, not knowing how many people were inside the house, how many guns. The other laser stayed steady.

She pointed toward the living room, the hardwood floor there lit by the fire. Chance nodded, crawled through the doorway, going for the Glock. A loud pop outside and the floodlight over the side door blew out, dropped the yard into darkness.

Kneeling, she pointed the shotgun at the side door, finger tight on the trigger. The laser began to move, playing across the wall above the living room doorway. But they'd have to get closer to have an angle on the room. They were having a conversation out there now. She could hear voices but not words.

Chance came back in, low to the floor, holding the Glock.

A round came through the side window, slammed into the wall beside the living room doorway. Glass rained down. Another followed it, tore off a piece of trim, the slug ricocheting into the living room. Then a flurry of shots, blowing out the rest of the side window, tearing through the curtain there, crisscrossing the room, punching into the walls. She could hear the clacking of a rifle bolt, a sound from the desert.

Silence then. The smell of gunpowder came through the broken side window. More footsteps in the yard there. She pointed at the door, and he nodded. That was the way they'd be coming in. He crawled backward into the living room, the Glock in front of him, the butt braced on the floor.

She slid along through broken glass, came up beside the table. Reaching up, she felt along the surface until her fingers touched loose shells. She drew down two, fed them into the receiver.

The only sound was the crackling of flames in the fireplace. She pushed the rest of the shells into the pockets of her jeans, then crawled across the floor to the far end of the kitchen, staying low as she passed the side door. When she reached the refrigerator, she stood, using it for cover, her back to the counter. From here, she was out of sight of both windows. She could hear a hissing from inside the refrigerator, thought of the beer cans there.

The laser blinked off. Seconds later, a bright flashlight beam came through a glass panel in the side door, lit up empty floor. She waved Chance back. He inched deeper into the doorway. The beam tracked across the kitchen but couldn't reach him. It made another circuit of the floor, then across to the space where she'd been, below the window. Then it went out.

She steadied the shotgun, guessing what they would do, thinking the kitchen was clear. Charge in force, with someone covering the front door as well, in case they tried to escape that way.

She was breathing fast, shallow. The shotgun felt heavier. Her hands were wet. She had to tuck the butt in hard against her shoulder to keep the barrel still.

The glass pane above the doorknob shattered, the butt of the flashlight coming through. Then a gloved hand pulled the last shards out of the frame and reached in, feeling around for the dead bolt. She held her breath.

The fingers closed on the lock, and as it began to twist open, she leaned across the refrigerator, held the muzzle of the shotgun a few inches from the gloved hand, and squeezed the trigger.

The muzzle flash lit the room. Wood splinters flew, blood spattered the linoleum. The man outside screamed, pulled his arm back through the window, and then Chance was firing from his prone position, three measured shots through the door.

She pivoted back, breathed, knew she had to press the advantage. She pumped, then swung around again, fired, blew out what was left of the door glass. Two men in the side yard, black jumpsuits, boots, no masks. One was dragging the other away, the man on the ground making an animal noise, holding what was left of his right arm. The man carrying him was big and blond, a rifle slung at his side. His chest was bulky beneath the jumpsuit. Body armor.

One-handed, he twisted the rifle on its sling, fired from the hip. The bullet went past her, and she ducked back. Three more rounds came through the door, hit the opposite wall. They weren't aimed, just a delaying tactic to get clear.

She pushed more shells into the shotgun, and when there was

no fourth shot from outside, she wheeled around and aimed through one of the blown-out door panes. But the two were already on the other side of the pickup, dropping down behind it for cover. She fired over their heads to keep them down, heard buckshot shred the branches behind them.

She pulled back behind the cover of the refrigerator, glass crunching under her boots. "You all right?"

"Yeah," Chance said. "How many?"

"Don't know. Two at least."

From up the gravel road, she heard the roar of an engine being revved. Through the front window, she saw headlights flash on, shine through the gate. The grind of metal on wood, the engine revving higher, and then a splintering crash as the vehicle came through. It swerved on the road, spraying gravel, then straightened. A big SUV with a heavy chrome pushbar.

"More of them," she said.

"Hicks?"

"I don't know. We have to split up, lead them away from the house, or we'll be trapped here. Where are the truck keys?"

He pulled a ring of keys from his pocket, sent them skittering across the floor. She bent, picked them up.

The headlights were coming fast. She kicked at what was left of the door. It flew open just as the two men broke from behind the pickup, ran toward the SUV, were silhouetted in its headlights. The wounded man had his good arm around the big one's neck, was being dragged along. She fired once at them, then at the SUV, knowing she couldn't hit anything from here, but wanting them to see the muzzle flash, to slow them down.

More shots to her right. Chance was firing through the front window at the SUV. It braked and swung to an angled stop across the road, blocking it, giving the running men cover. They hurried toward it, staying out of the headlights now. A rear door opened.

She ran for the pickup, tried the latch. Unlocked. She slid the shotgun across the bench seat, got behind the wheel, fumbled with the keys and got the engine started. There was a popping sound from behind, an unsilenced weapon. A round punched into the pickup's tailgate, then another.

She hit the gas, pulled away, tires spinning, narrowly missed one of the trees. She headed up the road toward the rear of the property, and now the SUV was moving again, coming fast.

With no headlights, she couldn't tell where the driveway ended and the dirt began. She swung past the barn, then onto the border of the soy field, the path there big enough for a tractor. The pickup bumped and rattled, jolting her in her seat. In the darkness, she could only guess where the back road was that led into the trees.

The SUV bore down on her, its big headlamps lighting the pickup's interior as bright as day. More popping, and the window behind her head starred. Something hit the dashboard.

She swerved right, then left, pulled the shotgun into her lap, balancing it on her knees, fed two more shells into the receiver. The SUV stayed on her. They couldn't let her get away. The men she'd shot at had worn vests but no balaclavas. Which meant they didn't care if anyone saw their faces, because they weren't going to leave anyone alive.

She spun the wheel, floored the gas, left the path and crashed onto the field, the pickup airborne for an instant, then coming down hard, jarring her. The truck mowed down the thigh-high plants, cutting a wide swath, the SUV closing in behind. Then there were no more plants, and the pickup plunged nose-first into an irrigation ditch, the impact slamming her into the steering wheel. She hit the gas, spun the wheel to the left, trying to get traction in the loose dirt. The truck lurched forward, rear tires spinning, and stalled out.

The SUV barreled toward her. No time to restart the engine, rock the truck free. She pushed open the door, jumped down, pointed the shotgun at the SUV, aiming two feet over the onrushing headlights. She fired, pumped and fired again. The SUV's left headlight went out, but it didn't slow. She fired again, and then there was no time, no room. She threw herself to the side, hit the ground hard, and the SUV surged over the edge of the ditch, all four wheels leaving the ground, and plowed into the side of the pickup.

The noise of it filled the night. She rolled away, lost the shotgun, was shrouded in dust. The SUV's engine roared, grew louder, then cut out.

The night grew quiet. She got to her knees, felt around until her fingers closed on the wooden stock of the shotgun. She coughed, rubbed a forearm across her eyes, trying to clear them. The SUV's lone headlamp pointed off at an angle, lighting up the dust cloud from within.

She spit out dirt, stood. The dust began to settle, and she saw the pickup was over on its right side. The SUV had T-boned the truck at a low angle, flipped it over, then come to rest that way, half in the ditch, the rear tires higher than the front.

She thumbed the last of the rounds into the shotgun, aimed it at the SUV's driver's side door, waiting for it to open. There was no movement inside. She could hear the engine ticking and cooling, the only sound now.

Finger tight on the trigger, she moved closer. The driver's side window was down, a man slumped over the wheel. She held the shotgun on him, came closer. Pellet holes riddled the windshield, and a fist-sized gap was blown out on the driver's side. There was blood on the back of his seat.

She used the shotgun muzzle to push him back off the steering wheel and the limp remains of the deflated air bag. The passenger seat was empty, the door there hanging open.

The driver had close-cropped hair, a pink scar on the side of his neck. He wore a camo jumpsuit. His eyes were half open. He'd caught a load of buckshot in the throat.

She let him slump forward again, circled the SUV, the shotgun up, butt tucked into her shoulder. It was a black Chevy Suburban, with Illinois plates. The rear passenger door was open as well. She pointed the shotgun inside. On the floor was the man she'd shot at the kitchen door. He was younger than the driver, his right arm a ruined mess. Dark blood had soaked through the carpet. With no tourniquet, he'd bled out. A silver cross and chain had slipped from the collar of his jumpsuit. They were dappled with blood.

She backed away from the SUV. At least two more of them out here somewhere. A figure came out of the house, started across the field, limping. Chance.

A groan behind her. She followed the noise, and there was the big blond one, facedown on the dirt path. A rifle stock stuck out from beneath him. There was blood in his hair. One of their wild shots must have grazed him as he ran for the Suburban. The collision had done the rest.

She knelt, keeping the shotgun on him, tugged at the rifle. It snagged for a moment, then came free. He moaned when she pulled it out from under him. It was an HK, like the ones they'd used in Nevada. She backed away, ejected the magazine, tossed the rifle out into the darkness. She patted him down for a side-arm, found none, left him there.

Back at the SUV, she got out her penlight, played the beam over the ground, saw the trail of crushed soy plants a few feet away. Blood in the dirt. Holding the penlight in a reverse grip in her left hand, she braced the shotgun barrel in the crook of her elbow.

She followed the blood trail through the plants, found Sandoval kneeling in a ditch holding his left arm. She shone the light on him, saw the compound fracture there, bone showing through. The side of his jumpsuit was soaked with blood. Some of it would be the driver's.

He looked up at her, smiled and shook his head. "I should have known, right?"

He dropped his right hand, came up with a dark automatic. She took a step forward, knocked it from his hand with the shotgun barrel. It landed in the dirt a few feet away. It was a SIG Sauer, no suppressor. He was the one who'd been shooting at the truck.

"Where's Hicks?" she said.

He cupped his broken arm again, looked at the SIG, then back at her, his chest rising and falling in ragged rhythm. Cracked ribs, she guessed.

She aimed the shotgun at him. "Is he here?"

"I should have done you out in the desert." He winced in pain. "Would have saved everybody a lot of trouble."

She heard dragging footsteps. Chance came up beside her, carrying the snub-nosed .38. His left jeans leg was dark with blood. Sandoval looked at him, spit on the ground at his feet.

"Where's Hicks?" she said again.

"You'll see him soon enough," Sandoval said.

"Who sent you out here?"

"We know who sent him," Chance said. "Why are we wasting time?"

She ignored him. "You want a doctor," she said, "you're going to have to tell me some things."

"Oh, yeah?" Sandoval said. "You gonna call a doctor for me? Get him to come out here, fix me up?"

"No, but I can take you someplace, a hospital. Drop you off outside. Then you're on your own. We do it soon enough, they might be able to save that arm."

"A hospital."

"How'd you find out about this place? From Sladden?"

Pain crossed his face again. "What do you think?" He looked at Chance. "Do what you're going to do, *maricón*. One way or another."

"Talk to me, and we'll get you to that hospital," she said. "Where's Hicks?"

He looked up at her, said, *"Que te den, puta."*

"Right," Chance said. "Semper fi, motherfucker." He raised the .38 and shot him in the head.

TWENTY-FOUR

When Hicks came through the front door, there were three suit-cases lined up in the foyer. He went through into the high-ceilinged living room. Katya came out of an adjoining hallway carrying a fourth suitcase, stopped when she saw him.

"Where is he?" he said. She nodded at the stairs.

He went up to the second floor, saw the light in Cota's study at the end of the hall. He stopped in the doorway. Cota had a wall safe open, was taking out bound packs of bills, stacking them on the desktop. The painting that had covered the safe was leaning against the wall. He was panicking, as Hicks had known he would. But it didn't matter now.

"What the fuck, Emile?"

Cota turned to look at him, then reached back into the safe.

"Where do you think you're going?" Hicks said. He'd almost been too late.

Cota put the last two packs on the desk. He looked pale, old.

"I was going to call you, tell you. I wasn't sure when you'd be back."

"You running out on me? I told you there's nothing to worry about. It's all been taken care of."

"You did. And I'm sure you're right." He limped toward the chair, sat down with a sigh. Hicks could see the sweat on his forehead. "But I was thinking, now might be an optimum time to take an overseas sabbatical. You should consider it as well."

"After all that happened? How do you think that'll look?"

Cota set his cane atop the desk. "Understood. But frankly, I'd feel more comfortable somewhere in Europe—Brussels, perhaps—until things calm down here, and our current trouble blows over."

"There's no trouble, not anymore," Hicks said. "They're all gone, or will be soon." Thinking about Sandoval and the others, on their way to Chance's farm. Or there already and done. And now just one thing left.

"You say. But can you really be sure?"

"Don't get squirrely on me, Emile. You'd be leaving me in a jam here. Or didn't you think about that?"

Cota didn't answer, took a leather valise from the floor, opened it on the desktop, and began to put the money inside.

"I half-expected as much," Hicks said. "That's why I'm here. Loose ends, right?"

Cota looked up at him. "What do you mean?"

"How much you have there?"

"Sixty thousand. Traveling money, that's all."

"What about the other safes in the house? There's money in all of them, right? How much were you going to take with you?"

Cota closed the valise, looked at him. "Randall, I'm grateful for all you've done on my behalf. I am. And I know it hasn't always been easy. On occasion I've asked you to do things you didn't want to."

"Yeah, you have."

"But I think we should go our separate ways for a little while, until things are calmer."

"They're calm now."

"Then as a precautionary measure."

"You were going to leave without me?"

"It's better if we travel separately. I think we can both agree on that. You want this"—he slid the valise across the desktop—"take it, it's yours."

Hicks laughed. "Sixty thousand?"

"Take it."

"You owe me a lot more than that, Emile."

"And I will pay you every penny of it."

"That's right," Hicks said. "You will."

Chance was silent in the car. She looked at his leg, said, "How bad is it?"

"Just a graze. I can take care of it myself."

They were on Highway 50, headed west, Crissa driving. They'd collected most of the weapons, disassembled them, put the parts into a duffel bag they'd dumped into a lake a few miles from the farm. She'd kept the Glock.

He'd taken what he could from the house, loaded a single suitcase. They'd left the four men where they lay, the blond one still alive out there in the field. There was nothing else to do.

"I'm sorry," she said.

"It wasn't your fault."

"I brought all this into your life."

"I made my choices. But this changes things. There's prints all over that house. Maybe other evidence, too, things I haven't even thought of."

"What will you do now?"

"Get Lynette. Figure out where to go next. Nothing back there was in my name, but the cops will talk to neighbors, people in town. They'll try to piece the whole thing together. And they will eventually. I've got enough money stashed away. We'll start again. Someplace else."

In her jeans pocket, the phone she'd taken from Sandoval started to buzz. She took it out. Hicks's number, the same one he'd been using. Sloppy.

"Is it him?" Chance said.

She nodded. "He's calling to see how it went."

"Let me talk to him."

She shook her head, pressed the TALK button, held the phone to her ear.

"Sandy?"

"No," she said.

Silence, then Hicks said, "I should have known."

"He said the same thing."

More silence. "He was a good man. We went back a long way."

She said nothing.

"So where does this leave us?" Hicks said.

"Where do you think?"

"We can still work this out."

"I don't think so." Chance was watching her.

"I didn't want things to go the way they did," Hicks said. "Any of it."

"You kept the same phone."

"Guess I didn't think I had anything to worry about anymore."

"You thought wrong."

"I'm not surprised, though. I knew there was a chance you'd walked away in Phoenix. I figured if you did, I'd be hearing from you again, one way or another."

"You owe me some money."

He laughed. "You'll have to take that up with the old man."

"I will."

"Let me know how that works out for you."

"Answer me one thing. Out in the desert. That driver, the one who ran, he was in on it, wasn't he?"

"What if I said yes?"

"Did you plan to kill him all along?"

"Not then. When it was all over, yeah. As a safety measure. But he forced our hand."

"Is that what all this has been? Safety measures?"

"Collateral damage."

"Cota know about all this, what you've done?"

"Does it matter now? He wanted his money, he didn't care how he got it. He looked the other way while I did the real work. Way it always was."

Chance reached for the phone. She shook her head.

Hicks said, "Sandy had some people with him."

"He did."

He took a breath. "All of them?"

"They called the play."

"God damn, girl."

When she didn't respond, he said, "So I guess we're the last ones standing. Funny how that worked out. No harm, no foul, though. I'm headed someplace where it's warm all year long, spend some of the old man's money. You should do the same. All in all, you didn't come out too bad."

"And you can leave it at that?"

"What else is there to do?"

"What about Sandoval?"

"Sandy was a soldier. He knew what he was getting into. We all did. Your people, too."

She took a breath. "You were wrong."

"About what?"

"About us. You and me. We're not alike. Not at all."

"No? Maybe you should think about that a little more."

"I did," she said, and ended the call.

"You should have let me talk to him," Chance said.

"There's nothing more to say." She opened the back of the phone, took out the SIM card, broke it in two, dropped the pieces out the window. Four miles later, she tossed the phone.

"So what now?" Chance said.

"We'll find a motel for tonight. Somewhere in Indiana, maybe. I'll feel better across the state line. We'll take a look at that leg, then get you on a train, plane, to Iowa, wherever. Then I've got some things to take care of."

"I'll come along."

"No," she said. "Not this time."

TWENTY-FIVE

The tennis court behind the house was the easiest way in. She used bolt cutters on the chain-link fence there, working by moonlight, the scrub pine hiding her from the neighboring houses. She wore a black windbreaker, black jeans, gloves, and sneakers.

A two-day drive out here, and she'd gotten what she needed along the way. Her rental car was parked up the hill, nosed into a stand of trees, hidden from the road.

When she'd cut an L in the chain-link, she slid through the gap, careful to avoid the jagged edges. Crouching there in the shadows of the court, she looked up at the house. Lights on the second and third floors, the ground floor dark. No sound but the faint splash of water from the fountain beyond the garden wall. She waited, watching for movement behind the windows. Nothing. She eased back a glove to look at her watch. Two A.M.

On the other side of the court was a chained and padlocked gate that led onto an enclosed patio. She crossed the court, used the bolt cutters on the chain, then unthreaded it from the fence posts. She left the chain and bolt cutters on the ground, opened the gate quietly and went through.

At the back door, she used strips of duct tape to cover the glass in one of the lower panes, then bumped it with an elbow. The glass cracked but stayed in place. She pulled gently on the loose ends of the tape, and the broken glass came away without a sound. She set the tape down, plucked the last glass fragments from the frame, then waited, listening for any sounds inside the house. Somewhere in the hills, a coyote called.

A long count of sixty, and only silence. She reached in then, felt around for the dead bolt, unlocked it. The door opened inward. No chain. Staying low, she slid in, eased the door shut behind her, waiting for an alarm.

When a minute had passed in silence, she took the Glock from her belt, then got out the penlight, switched it on.

It was a concrete-floored pantry, a washer and dryer on one side of the room. On the other, a meat freezer and shelves stocked with canned foods. On the wall to her right was a keyboard for the alarm system. All the lights were dark. The system had been disarmed.

She turned off the penlight, tried the door on the other side of the pantry. It was unlocked, led into a kitchen. With the Glock at her side, she went through, listening. Faint TV noise from an upper floor, nothing else.

She walked the ground-floor rooms, using the penlight only when she had to. When she was sure the downstairs was empty, she went through the big living room and up the marble staircase to the second floor. The room with the fireplace was empty, but there were lights on in the hallway. A door on the right was ajar, where the TV noise was coming from. At the end of the hall, another open door, a dimly lit room inside.

She stopped at the first door, eased it open with a shoulder. It was a bedroom, lit by a single lamp on a nightstand. On the wall, a flat-screen TV showing a black-and-white movie, the sound turned low.

Katya lay in the bed, naked, sheets tangled around her fleshy legs. Her wrists were tied to the bedposts with red silken scarves. Another was around her neck, deep in the flesh there. She was facing away from the door, her eyes half open, her face purple and swollen.

Crissa backed out of the room, moved down the carpeted hallway. The room at the end was a study. Bookshelves against the walls, an antique globe on a wooden stand, a desk lamp the only light. Near the desk, a painting of a clipper ship hung crooked on the wall.

She stepped in, the Glock in a two-handed grip, pointing at shadows. The room was empty.

At the desk, she lowered the gun, eased the painting aside. As she'd expected, there was a wall safe there, open a half inch. She lifted the painting off its hook, set it on the desk. Inside the safe were documents, a burgundy British passport, empty shelves.

She went back down the hall, then up the stairs to the next floor. A cool breeze blew through the corridor. She followed it into the room with the big oak table. The French doors to the balcony were open, the curtains there shifting in the breeze.

She aimed the Glock at the French doors, waiting for someone to come through them. She gave it a count of fifty, then went through the doors, gun up. The balcony was empty. The key lights were on in the gardens below, and she could hear the whisper of the fountain. Her foot hit something. Cota's cane. She went to the marble railing, looked down.

Cota lay faceup on the flagstones three floors below, eyes open. One leg was twisted up under him, a hand outstretched as if pointing to the fountain, the statue of the winged man. Blood had pooled beneath his head.

She saw then how it was supposed to look. Cota killing the maid, then going off the balcony himself. A murder and a suicide. Everything resolved, and no witnesses. Hicks at work, closing the pipeline on his own.

There was no sense trying to find his Venice apartment, waiting for him to show up. He'd be far away from Los Angeles by now, with whatever he'd taken from Cota. It was over.

Back inside, she retraced her steps, let herself out onto the patio. She picked up the bolt cutters, went back the way she'd come.

It took her three days to drive back to New Jersey. She got home in the middle of the night, exhausted and aching. When she woke the next day, after twelve hours of what felt like drugged sleep, the sun was already low in the west. She made coffee, took it out on the deck, called Rathka.

"You're back, I hope," he said.

"I am."

"I was worried."

"Things are settled, for now."

"Good. I have some investment ideas for your most recent deposit. I think you'll approve."

"I'm sure I will."

"And you said there's more to come?"

"No," she said. "Things went a different way."

He took a moment to process that. "Sorry to hear it. You should come by someday soon. We can take a look at your portfolio. See what you like, what you don't like."

"I trust you."

"Any fallout from your recent trip we need to discuss?"

"Nothing that affects you."

She thought of what Hicks had said on the phone. Had he really gone somewhere warm, or was that just misdirection? There would be no percentage in his staying around. He had all the money he was going to get, had burned all his bridges. She was no threat to him now, and he knew it.

"One other thing," she said. "I think I'd like to do some traveling soon. Change of scenery."

"No work involved?"

"No."

"That's good. I've been hoping you'd take some R&R. Happy to help. What did you have in mind?"

"I don't know. Europe, maybe. I've never been there. I've always wondered what Paris was like."

"You'll love it. Monique can set that up for you, four-star all the way."

"No," she said. "An apartment maybe, something simple. A place I can live for a while without attracting attention."

"How long were you thinking?"

"I'm not sure. A couple months maybe, then I'll decide. If I get bored before that, I'll come home, figure something else out."

"I'm glad to hear you talking this way. That you're giving some other things a rest."

"I might make a trip to Texas first. Let him know what's going on."

"My advice? Make it a quick one. Don't get distracted, change your mind about going away."

"We'll see how it plays."

"Give him my best," Rathka said. "And tell him we haven't given up."

"He knows that. But I'll tell him anyway."

"Let me look into these other issues, get back to you. I have a friend, a publisher, who knows Paris like she was born there. I'm sure we can come up with something that'll work for you, something off the tourist path."

"Thanks."

"In the meantime, you should come by the office. Monique'll make you an espresso. I'll show you the latest pictures of the twins. They just turned eight."

"Maybe I will," she said.

The faces came to her that night, as she knew they would. Struggling to sleep, the Lunesta not working, she'd see them again. A man with his throat torn open by buckshot. A blood-spattered silver cross. Sandoval in a ditch, eyes dull, looking up at the night sky, his life draining into the dirt beneath him. Then the desert again. The snapping of rifle bolts. Four men facedown, motionless.

Too much blood this time, too much pain. And none of it worth it.

When the bedside clock said five A.M., she gave up, took a bottle of wine out on the deck. She poured a glass, sat on the steps, arms wrapped around herself, listening to the wind and the water.

Home again, she thought. A different world. A different life.

Dawn was breaking, a red sun rising over the ocean, when she went back inside, carrying the glass and the empty bottle. She slept then, sprawled atop the sheets in sweats and T-shirt, the Glock on the nightstand, pale light coming through the windows. She didn't dream.

TWENTY-SIX

She woke at noon, her mouth dry, washed down two aspirin with a full bottle of water. They barely touched her headache.

Most of what was in the refrigerator had gone bad while she'd been away. She threw out almost everything, made a list of what she'd need at the store. Then she dropped the rental off at an agency office in Ocean Township, took a cab home, got her own leased Ford out of the garage she kept two blocks from her house. At the post office, she went though two weeks of mail. Utility bills, junk mail solicitations, and two business envelopes from Rathka's office.

She threw away the junk, opened the letters at a side counter. Each had a check for fifteen thousand, yields from various investments. She'd deposit each in a separate bank.

The afternoon was already turning gray, clouds moving in. At the grocery store, she replaced what she'd thrown away, paused at the entrance to the adjoining liquor store. Her head still ached, but she knew she'd have to drink again tonight if she hoped to sleep.

She bought a bottle of Medoc, told herself she'd only have a glass. Knew she was fooling herself. This would grow to be a problem if she let it.

Back at the house, she put on a red and black Puma tracksuit, did the mile run along the inlet and into Belmar, then back, panting and nauseous all the way. But her head had begun to clear, and by the time she reached the house she had sweated most of the alcohol out of her system.

The wind was picking up outside, rattling the windows, slicing whitecaps on the inlet. She wasn't hungry, but knew she would feel better with something in her stomach. For dinner, she cooked a hamburger steak, microwave french fries. She ate standing at the kitchen counter, looked over at the bottle of wine on the table. A glass or two afterward, that would be it.

The air was thick with humidity, and there was a deep ache in her hip. She found two pain pills left in a bottle in the medicine cabinet and took one with a palmful of water from the faucet.

In the living room, she turned on the radio, opened the bottle of wine and got a glass from the cabinet. She sat on the couch, listened to a Handel concerto she recognized but couldn't name. With her third glass of wine, she felt the tension of the last few weeks starting to fall away.

She took the bottle and glass out onto the deck, left the sliding glass door open, sat on the steps, the music drifting out around her. Night now, but still warm, the air heavy. The houses on both sides of hers were dark. To the east, over the ocean, lightning pulsed on the horizon.

She drank wine, watched the oncoming storm. The wind grew

stronger, water lapping rhythmically against her dock. She filled her glass again, saw the bottle was nearly empty.

So much for one glass, she thought. You need to get a handle on this before it gets bad.

The first raindrops came then, thick and warm. Call it a night, she thought, and start making some changes tomorrow.

The rain picked up, the thunder closer. She got up, tired and sore, carried the bottle and glass inside, shut the sliding door against the wind and the night.

The smell woke her. The scent of rain, of the sea, of night on the water. It pulled her out of a dream in which she was sinking into an immense darkness, trying to swim back to a surface miles above.

She opened her eyes. Rain drummed steadily on the roof, a lulling sound that had helped ease her into sleep. On the nightstand, the clock read three fifteen. The radio still played softly in the living room. She'd left it on when she'd fallen asleep.

She sat up, saw the figure by her bed, a blacker shadow in the darkness. She pushed away covers, reached for the Glock on the nightstand, knocked over the empty wine bottle there. Her hand closed around the gun, and she pointed it at the shadow, finger on the trigger. It felt wrong, the balance and weight off.

The nightstand lamp went on, and Hicks was sitting there, in a chair beside the bed, dripping wet. He held up the Glock's magazine so she could see it, put it on the nightstand. "You sleep sound."

She squeezed the trigger. It depressed halfway, stopped.

"I took the round in the chamber, too," he said. "Knew you'd have one there."

Thunder in the distance. The rain on the roof grew louder. She kept the Glock steady.

"That alarm company ripped you off," he said. "Once I got into your basement from outside, it only took about ten minutes to figure out how to override the whole thing. I were you, I'd ask for your money back."

She slid away from him to the other side of the bed, the gun still up, untangled her legs from the covers.

"Door's right there," he said. "Think you can make it?"

She came off the bed, stood. She wore sweatpants and a T shirt. The hardwood floor was cold beneath her bare feet.

He picked up the bottle, set it back on the nightstand. "Drinking to forget? How's that working out for you?"

She stayed where she was, keeping the bed between them. She could use the Glock as a club if she had to, but from where he sat he blocked the open door. In the hallway beyond, she could see the gleam of wet footprints on the floor.

"See, that gun's just a hunk of metal now," he said. "It's useless. But this"—he reached down into his boot, came up with a wood-handled ice pick—"is always loaded. It's as primitive as it gets. Silent, too."

She thought of Sladden, the patchwork of holes in his flesh, the final entry wound at the base of his skull.

"How did you find me?" she said.

"Your friend in Kansas City. On one of his laptops he had a post box number and a zip code for you. The hard drive was password protected, but one of my guys cracked it. The entry was half-ass coded, and under a different name, but it wasn't hard to figure out."

She took a step to the left. He watched her.

"Long odds, but it was worth a shot," he said. "I drove all the way out here, found that post office. Tough part was the waiting. I sat in that parking lot across the street for three days, pissing into an iced-tea bottle, waiting for you to come along and check your mail. Not knowing if you ever would, or if you even lived around here anymore. I got lucky, I guess."

"What do you want?"

"Not sure, exactly. If all I'd wanted was to kill you, I'd have done it while you were still asleep. Just pushed this thing through an ear canal and into your brain. You'd never know what hit you. It would have been easy for me that way. Easy for you, too."

"Why didn't you?"

"I don't know. Maybe I just wanted to look into your eyes again, one last time."

She thought about the .32 in its holster, clipped beneath the bed, only inches from his leg. But no way to reach it from here.

She lowered the Glock. She could throw it, aim for his head, hope to stun him enough to get past him and through the door.

He stood up then, as if he knew what she was thinking, pushed the chair back. He wore a black field jacket over a dark crew-neck sweater, the chest bulky, the vest beneath showing through. He took the magazine from the nightstand, pocketed it.

"I guess I was looking for a little closure, too," he said. "And maybe some revenge."

"For Sandoval?"

"Who pulled the trigger on him? You or Chance?"

"Does it matter?"

"I guess not. Since when I'm done with you, I'll go find him as well. I'll square it, one way or another."

"You didn't have to do what you did. None of us would have talked."

"Couldn't take the chance. The old man wasn't too clear with me on numbers, but I'm guessing he stood to make a good twenty million on that deal. He promised me a nice piece of it. We didn't want someone fucking things up six months down the line, giving everybody up to get out of some other bullshit charge."

"That wouldn't have happened."

"There was only one way to make sure."

"Didn't do him much good in the long run, though, did it?" she said. "I was out at the house. I saw what you did."

He sighed. "Yeah, that was *regrettable,* as he might say. But our partnership was a losing proposition, for me at least. Even with all I did for him, he was never going to see me as anything but an employee. More I thought about it, more I realized it would never work out."

She rounded the foot of the bed.

"If you think you can make it," he said, "go for it."

From this angle, she could see down the hallway to the living room. The vertical blinds over the sliding glass door were bunched together, pushed aside. Rain was sheeting against the glass. So that was the way he'd come in. He'd disabled the alarm, forced the lock, and she'd slept through it all.

"Another reason," he said. "I figured you had some cash stashed here somewhere. A safe maybe. I got a little something from Emile. Not as much as I could have if I'd played it better, unfortunately. But sometimes you just have to cut your losses. So I could use a little more traveling money before I hit the road."

"There's no cash here."

"Maybe I'll just poke around a little anyway, find out."

He took a pair of steel handcuffs from his jacket pocket, threw them on the bed. "Why don't you go ahead and put those on?"

"No chance."

"I could make you."

"You could try."

He grinned at that, came around the bed fast. She threw the gun at his face, but he saw it coming, raised his left arm, knocked it aside. She lunged for the door, and he was on her before she reached it, his left arm around her throat.

They went through the open doorway together, his weight bringing them down hard in the hallway. The impact drove the breath out of her. She tried to push him away, and he swung atop her, the ice pick in his right hand. She went for his eyes.

"Stop it," he said. He batted her hands away. "Just fucking stop it."

He pressed the point of the ice pick to her cheek. She twisted away from it, got her right hand on his throat, plunged her thumb into the soft space beneath his Adam's apple. With her left hand, she caught his right wrist, tried to push the ice pick away from her face.

He knocked her hand from his throat, then pulled his right hand free of her grip. She jabbed at his eyes again, and he caught her throat with his left hand, lifted her head and drove it back down into the floor. Sparks flashed at the edge of her vision. He raised the ice pick high, his left hand still on her throat, pinning her.

"This what you want?" His voice was hoarse. "This the way you want it to go?"

She looked at his eyes, knew then he'd made his decision, knew what she had to do.

The ice pick flashed down. She raised her left hand, palm out. Felt the impact, and then the pain as the blade pierced her hand. The point came through the other side.

An electric shock ran up her arm. He looked at her hand, as if surprised by what he'd done. But she was already moving, squirming, swinging her hips out from under him. He let go of the ice pick, and this time she had the leverage, got her center of gravity up and over. She twisted atop him, drove her forehead into his nose, once, twice.

She scrambled off him, onto her feet, moving back toward the bedroom, dizzy. Without thinking, she pulled the ice pick from her hand, tossed it aside. Just numbness there now. She went through the bedroom door, and then his hand was around her ankle, and she was going down hard, face-first.

Her chin hit the floor, her head snapping back, and for an instant everything went red. Instinct got her hands under her, tried to push the floor away, and sudden pain tore through her left palm, made her cry out. He held her leg tight, and she twisted onto her back, kicked at him with a bare heel, hit his forehead. Blood was coming from his nose. She kicked again, and he swatted her foot away, starting to climb up her, pinning her with his weight. She tried to buck him off, couldn't. She looked up and saw the holster clipped to the bedsprings, swept her right hand toward it. It was still a foot away, unreachable.

His left forearm came down across her throat, his weight behind it. She punched at him with her right hand, aiming for the ruined nose, hit his cheekbone instead.

"Stop fighting me, goddammit," he said. "Stop . . . fighting."

Sparks in her vision again, his arm on her throat like an iron bar, bearing down. She raised her hips, trying to push herself closer toward the bed, her bloody left hand sliding on the wood.

Her vision seemed to narrow, constrict. His face was close to hers, red with exertion, grinning. A drop of sweat fell from his forehead to her lips. He gripped his left wrist with his right hand, pushed down. She felt something start to give way in her throat. She reached back with her right hand, felt the bed, the frame, then the springs.

All his weight on her now. The hardness of the vest beneath his sweater as he pressed into her, no space between their bodies, his face close enough she felt his hot breath. Her vision began to blur. Her fingers touched cool metal, plastic. The gun.

She drew it out, pressed the muzzle into his armpit, feeling for where the vest ended. Squeezed the trigger.

A flat crack, muffled by cloth and flesh. He cried out, rolled off her, and she fired again, the bullet hitting the wall behind him. She moved in the other direction, got her feet under her, tried to stand but couldn't find her balance. She fell back against the nightstand, knocked the lamp over, and he was up and moving fast through the doorway, into the hall. She fired at his back, heard his breath go out as the round hit his vest, and then he was gone.

She slumped against the bed, rested there for a moment, aiming the Tomcat into the darkness of the hall. Blood was in her mouth, and her tongue found a cut on the inside of her cheek, a loose tooth. She tried to steady herself, catch her breath, waiting for him to come back through the door again.

Her left hand throbbed. It was already swelling, the puffed

flesh almost hiding the red hole in her palm. She held it close to her side, went into the hall. She could hear him breathing in the darkness.

She found the hall light switch, used the muzzle of the .32 to flip it. The track lighting went on.

He was on his knees in the living room, back to her, panting, head down, right arm draped over the back of a chair for support. Blood drops led from the hallway to where he knelt. Beyond him, the glass door rattled as rain blew against it. Thunder boomed outside.

She made a wide circle around him, went to the glass door. Rain was pebbling the inlet. The yard was dark and empty. Tied to the dock was a small dinghy, bobbing on the water.

He coughed, wheezed, looked up at her. "I think you hit a lung."

"Are you alone?"

He coughed again, blood on his lips, then tried to smile at her. "I'm serious. You fucked me up."

"You shouldn't have come back."

"Too late for that now." He rose unsteadily to his feet, leaning on the chair.

She pointed the gun at him. "Don't."

He lowered his head, ran toward her. She fired, missed, and then he was on her, arms wrapped around her waist, lifting her, and they were going backward. Her back hit the blinds, the door, and then the resistance was gone, the glass exploding around them, and she was on her back in the rain, the Tomcat gone, Hicks on top of her again. They rolled down the slick steps and onto the grass. She got her knees up between them, pushed him away, kicked with both feet. He flew back, landed in a sitting position. She twisted, and there was the Tomcat, lying in the wet grass.

He rolled to his feet, came at her, teeth showing, and she grabbed for the gun, got hold of it, turned back just as he reached her, and shot him twice in the face.

TWENTY-SEVEN

She lay back on the grass, breathing hard, watching the rain come down. The slide of the Tomcat had locked back. She dropped the gun on the grass, got to her feet, almost fell, and had to sit on the steps. Hicks wasn't moving. He was on his back, one leg bent under him.

The shots hadn't been loud, had been lost in the wind and rain. No lights had gone on in any of the other houses. Her own deck was dark. She looked up and saw that the bulb for the motion sensor light was missing.

Thunder boomed again. She managed to stand, found the two shell casings, went back up on the deck. All that remained of this half of the door was the frame. There were scratch marks around the lock where he'd forced it.

Stepping carefully over broken glass, she pushed the bent blinds aside, went in, put the gun and casings on the counter.

There was always the chance someone had heard the struggle, called the police, so she had to move fast. The body first.

In the bedroom, she peeled off her wet and bloody clothes, put on jeans and a sweater, a dark windbreaker, struggling to do it one-handed. Her left palm was swollen, the fingers curled into a claw, but the bleeding had stopped.

She went back out into the rain. He hadn't moved. She turned out his pockets, found car keys, a wallet, the magazine for the Glock, and a folding knife with a four-inch blade. She put them in her jacket, then caught him under the armpits, gripping with her left hand as well as she could. She dragged him down the lawn and onto the dock.

The dinghy was riding high in the water, the inlet swollen by the rain. Halfway toward the ocean, on the other side of the inlet, an outfall pipe protruded from the seawall. Gushing storm water churned the surface there, the current picking up speed as it ran seaward.

She caught the rope, pulled the boat closer until it was directly below the dock, scraping against a piling. The dinghy was old, unpainted. He might have stolen it from any number of houses on the inlet. Rainwater had gathered in the bottom.

Headlights passed across the bridge. She stayed low until they were gone, then caught Hicks's jacket, turned him over and pushed. He rolled off the dock and into the dinghy, his head thumping against the gunwale. He landed faceup. The boat rolled as if it would capsize, then steadied.

There was a single oar in the dinghy. Lying on the dock, she reached down with her right hand, stretched, caught the oar and dragged it up beside her. She had to rest then, her breath coming in gasps. A flash of lightning showed her Hicks's ruined face, lit as if by daylight.

She had to keep moving. If the rain kept up like this, it might sink the dinghy too close to the house. She used his knife to cut the rope, threw the loose ends into the dinghy, then tossed the blade out into the water.

The oar was harder to handle, but she got the flat end against the transom, pushed. The boat slid away from the dock, toward the center of the inlet. She tossed the oar down into it. It fell across Hicks's chest.

She sat there in the rain, watched the dinghy drift out, already listing to the side. It slowed to a stop about ten feet from the dock, sitting heavy in the water. Then it did a lazy circle as another current caught it, pushed it farther out. It began to move faster. As it neared the seawall, the water sluicing from the outfall pipe drove it on. It sat lower in the water now, but if she was lucky, it would reach the ocean before it sank or capsized. The vest would drag the body down.

There was nothing more she could do. She watched the boat vanish into the darkness, then went back inside.

Water was puddled on the living room floor. She threw towels down to soak it up, then got a sponge, scrubbed at the still-damp blood spots on the hardwood floor. There weren't many. Most of the bleeding from his gunshot wound had stayed inside the vest.

When she was done, she got a pillowcase from the bed. Into it went all the shell casings, then the disassembled parts of the Tomcat and the Glock, the magazines, the handcuffs, and the ice pick. She rinsed her hand clean in the bathroom sink, then poured hydrogen peroxide over the wound, grinding her teeth at the pain. She wrapped it as best she could with gauze and surgical tape.

Wind was rattling the vertical blinds. There was little she could do about the door tonight. She pulled one of the wrought-iron chairs inside, laid it on its side in the puddled water and broken glass. If police showed up at her door before morning, her story would be that the wind had driven the chair through the door.

She got an extra shower curtain from the pantry, a staple gun from beneath the sink. Holding the curtain up with her bad hand, she managed to keep it in place over the trim long enough to use the staple gun across the top and down the side. When she was done, the curtain moved like a bellows, the wind pulling at the edges, but it held, and no more water came in.

Exhausted, she sat down at the kitchen table, opened his wallet. Two hundred dollars in twenties, a California driver's license, credit cards. The wallet went into the pillowcase. She kept the money.

She found the car a few blocks away, in a cul-de-sac that dead-ended at the inlet. It was a Dodge Avenger with Tennessee plates, likely stolen. She knew he'd have a vehicle close by, couldn't have come far in the dinghy in that weather.

She parked her own car on a side street, carried the pillowcase to the Dodge, locked it in the trunk, then got behind the wheel and started the engine. She wore a pair of knit wool gloves, had managed to pull the material over her swollen left hand. The pain was a steady throbbing, keeping her awake, keeping her moving.

She drove a half mile west, paralleling the inlet, then pulled into the empty lot of a dark seafood restaurant. She parked in back, turned the lights off but left the engine running, got the pillowcase from the trunk.

There was a dock here for customers who came by boat. It ran fifty feet out into the inlet, ended on a floating platform. All the slips were empty.

She went out to the platform, the rain beating down on her, the floating dock unsteady beneath her feet. She tossed the shell casings and gun parts as far as she could, heard them splash, threw the handcuffs and ice pick out after them, then went back to the car.

She drove three towns north to Asbury Park, wipers thumping. She parked on an empty street near a housing project, left the keys in the ignition, took the pillowcase. The wallet went into a storm drain, the pillowcase into a Dumpster she passed. Walking toward the center of town, she saw the lights of the all-night taxi office next to the train station. She got a cab back to where her car was parked, paid with one of Hicks's twenties. Five minutes later, she was home.

TWENTY-EIGHT

The sun was high over the ocean, the water calm and flat. She stood on the boardwalk, looking out over the jetty at the mouth of the inlet. A light breeze blew in off the water. Gulls wheeled above her.

She was sore all over. Her hand was bandaged, but the swelling had gone down. She'd been to a walk-in clinic that morning, told the doctor she'd stabbed herself while defrosting her freezer, was chipping away at ice when the pick slipped.

He'd asked about the bruises on the throat, why her voice was hoarse, and she'd told him she'd run into a clothesline in her backyard two days before. He'd been skeptical, but hadn't asked any more questions, had given her a prescription for antibiotics and painkillers. The pick had gone through cleanly, without nicking any tendons. Her fingers were stiff, but she could move them.

Contractors were at the house now, replacing the glass door. She'd called them first thing in the morning, told them the storm had blown a deck chair through the glass. They'd had a replacement door in stock, would be done by the time she went back. In the bedroom, she'd moved a dresser to cover the bullet hole in the wall. There were no other signs of what had happened in the night.

She took out the phone she'd bought that morning, held it awkwardly in her bandaged hand, called Chance. When his voice mail picked up, she said, "It's me," and hung up. Two minutes later, her phone buzzed

"Where are you?" he said.

"Home."

"What's wrong with your voice?"

"Nothing. It'll pass. How's the leg?"

"Cleaned it out, patched it up myself. Another scar, but what's new?"

"How'd it go when you got there?"

"A little rough. Told her what I could. None of it seemed to have made much difference, though. I'd promised her once that I was out of it, you know? And she believed me."

"I'm sorry."

"She'll come around. We'll find someplace. Maybe another farm if we're lucky, if I can find someone to carry the paper."

"You need some short-term money, let me know," she said. "We'll work it out."

"Should be all right for a while. I've already cleared out my Ohio accounts. I've got some more stashed away, here and there. That last deposit helped. There won't be any repercussions from that, will there?"

"No, I don't think so."

"So what are you not telling me?"

She flexed the fingers of her left hand, felt the dull ache there. "There was a little drama last night. I had a visitor."

"Who?"

"Our military friend."

He took a breath. "How did it go?"

"He won't be coming back."

A pause on the line, then, "And you're all right?"

"Yes."

"What about his employer?"

"He dealt with that himself. There won't be any blowback."

"So we're clear?"

"We are."

She heard him exhale. "They did some damage, though, to both of us."

"They did."

"I need to rebuild some things. My life had a structure before all this. That's gone. And what I've got now won't last forever. Comes down to it, who knows, a year from now, I might need some work."

"I thought you were out of it?"

"I thought so, too."

Got the taste for it back, she thought. Even with all that had happened. She watched waves roll in to the beach, sunlight sparkling on the water.

"I'll keep that in mind," she said. "But I think I'm taking a break myself. Maybe do some traveling."

"How long?"

"I don't know. I just feel like I need a change, that things are different now."

"What happened this time, it wasn't your fault."

"I'm not so sure about that."

"I mean, nobody could have predicted it, right? Like you always say, nothing for it. So something comes along a year from now, maybe eighteen months, you need to give me a call."

"All right," she said.

"And maybe I'll see you then."

"Maybe you will," she said.

She was at the gate at Newark Airport, waiting for her flight to San Antonio to be called, carry-on bag at her feet, when her cell buzzed. Rathka.

"I found a place I think you'll like," he said. "A little town just outside Paris. Another one of my clients owns it, was renting it out, but it's empty now. And he won't be going back any time soon."

"Legal problems?"

"You could say that. Strictly white-collar, though. Pension fund issues. Won't go to trial until next year, if it goes to trial at all. In the meantime, he's hoping to generate some income."

"To pay your bill?"

"The best never comes cheap. But you don't have to worry about any of that. The title's clean. Not much to the place, one bedroom, and it's old. But it's quiet, from what I understand. Might suit your needs. I can get you some pictures."

"No need," she said. "Make the deal. Give him three months rent in advance, starting next month. Then we'll see what happens."

Through the plate-glass window, she could see her plane drawing up to the jetway. Beyond it, in the distance, the Manhattan skyline.

"Given all that's transpired recently," he said, "what are your plans in the meantime?"

"Heading south to see our friend."

"Is that wise?"

"What do you mean?"

"Maybe you should take that time-out sooner rather than later. Stay clear of all this for a while. You've been putting a lot of money away the last couple of years. It's time you started enjoying some of it, isn't it? Otherwise, what's the point?"

"I have responsibilities."

"Nothing that can't be handled long-distance. That's what I'm here for, why you pay me."

Passengers were coming through the gate now, filing off the plane. She looked at the boarding pass in her bandaged hand, the tattoo on her wrist just below it. She thought about what Wayne had said the last time she saw him. *You shouldn't have to live like that. You deserve better.*

"You still there?" Rathka said.

"Yeah."

"That place is ready now. I can have Monique book you a flight this week, tomorrow if you want. Why waste time?"

"I'll think about it."

"Do."

The gate attendant was calling out seating groups over the PA. The outgoing passengers began to queue up in separate lines. The first group started through the gate and down the jetway, the ticket reader beeping as the attendant scanned their boarding passes.

She took a deep breath, looked out the window again. *Someday, you're going to have to make a choice.*

"In the meantime," Rathka was saying, "I'll move some money around for you, keep it liquid, accessible. The dollar's getting stronger over there, you'll do all right."

The last group was heading down the jetway, the gate area almost empty now.

"All you have to do is say the word," he said. "I can put the whole thing in motion tomorrow."

Final boarding call. The gate attendant looked over at her.

"Well?" Rathka said.

"Do it," she said, and ended the call.

As the plane banked east, she looked out the window. Nothing but ocean below.

In the First Class seat beside her, a businessman in his forties was typing on a laptop. The flight attendant came back with their drinks, red wine for her, a gin and tonic for him.

"Long flight," he said.

She looked at him. He was tanned, his black hair shot through with gray. He'd taken off his suit jacket and loosened his tie, was using the folded jacket as a rest for the laptop. She saw the wedding ring on his left hand.

"Sorry?" she said. She put the wineglass on her tray table.

"It's a long trip," he said. "I used to do it once a month. Never got used to it. Eight hours is about three hours too long for me. You get over to the Continent much?"

"I've never been," she said. "First time."

"Business?"

"No."

"Family there?"

She shook her head.

"Just traveling on your own?"

"That's right."

"Good for you. Best way to do it sometimes. You speak any French?"

"No."

"You'll be fine. 'Please' and 'thank you' get you pretty far in any country. You'll find you pick up what you need pretty quickly."

"I hope so."

He nodded at her bandaged hand. "That looks painful."

"Not so much anymore."

"What happened?"

"Kitchen accident."

"You must have a dangerous kitchen."

The plane began to bank again. To the west, the sunset was painting the ocean bloodred.

"Seriously," he said. "You'll love it there, I'm sure. Especially if you've never been."

She didn't respond, ran her thumb over the tattoo on her wrist.

"Sometimes it's the scariest things that pay off the best," he said. "Anything worthwhile in life comes with an element of uncertainty to it, risk. At least that's what I've always found."

"You may be right."

"Well, then," he said. "Here's to new adventures."

She touched her glass to his, drank, then looked out the window again. The water was darkening with the coming night.

She finished her wine, set the glass down. She was tired now, and suddenly sad, for no reason she knew. He saw it in her, went back to his laptop.

She'd figure it out as she went, she thought. What to do

tomorrow, the day after that, the weeks and months that would follow. Where it would all lead her.

She put her head back, closed her eyes, and flew on into darkness.